MW01103608

AFTER CLAIRE

In Search of a Habitable Life

A NOVEL

JOHN R. WALLIS

ISBN 978-1-66780-651-8 (Print)
ISBN 978-1-66780-652-5 (eBook)

PART ONE

CHAPTER ONE

"Did Mommy go to heaven right away, or only just now?" Allie's question surprised me out of a trance of disbelief. Claire had just been lowered into the ground and a large part of my mind was still trying to go back to the week before, when she was still alive.

I had no idea how to answer my daughter. But there was something urgent in her voice, and in her eyes. I drew her close with a hand on her shoulder. "Right away," I whispered. "Sometimes, I can almost see her face in the clouds."

Allie took a brief, furtive glance toward the sky, her blue eyes lit with a momentary flicker of light. Then she looked down at the carefully manicured ground, her features slackening. "Can we go home now?" she asked, her voice so frail I wanted to take her in my arms.

But how could I offer her comfort when it was I who had taken Claire from her? From us.

I asked Allie if she wanted to cast a handful of dirt into the grave as some were doing—Claire's parents, Claire's sister, a few friends and colleagues where Claire had taught high school math. Allie looked up at me, her straw-colored hair ruffling in the breeze. "No. I just want to go home."

Going home suited me, too. Everyone at the graveside, everyone except Allie that is, knew exactly how Claire had died; knew about the citation I'd gotten for reckless driving. On the way to the funeral that morning, I'd hoped someone might let me know—with a word or touch or kind regard—that they understood my grief was different than theirs, that the pain in my heart was accompanied by near suffocating guilt. No one had. By the time Allie was ready to leave, the collective judgement of everyone present, communicated with downcast eyes and furrowed brows, had pissed me off to the point where I thought about going up to Claire's mother and telling her I hadn't *meant* to kill Claire.

I didn't do that, of course, It was my own shame, much more than Marge's disapproval, that held me in its punishing grip, and to confront Marge in such a ridiculous way would only feed its fury.

I took Allie's hand and we left together, Allie walking gracefully in spite of what she must be feeling, in spite of being so tall for her age and too thin, both of us returning to a home where we would have to learn how to live all over again. From scratch, as they say. And as we walked toward the car, a question burned in my mind like the smoldering underbrush of a fire I feared might consume us both.

What would happen between us when Allie learned the precise circumstances of her mother's death?

• • •

Weeks later I walked into Allie's bedroom to wake her for school. Her hair was golden in the early morning light, her forehead and cheeks smooth and untroubled. I was tempted to leave her to her dreams; it was Claire's birthday after all, and I feared what heartbreak this day might bring. Allie stirred in the bed. The way the bridge of her nose gave way to closely spaced eyes reminded me so much of Claire I had to look away. It occurred to me then that Claire would be forever *there* in Allie's face. And in her hands, the way her littlest finger bent inward at the tip, just like Claire's

I'd never before imagined that the genetic imprint a parent left on a child could be so painful.

"Time to get up, Daddy?" Allie's small, high voice startled me out of my thoughts.

"Yes it is, Sweetpea. The sun's come up again, after all." I'd meant this as a joke, but Allie grimaced her disapproval, and it hurt.

The day before, Allie had overheard two older girls talking about how one day the sun will burn itself out. She'd asked her fourth-grade teacher if this was true and the teacher confirmed it. When Allie told me later that day what she'd learned, how one day even the sun will die, her voice had risen to a frantic pitch. "When that happens, Daddy, there'll be no more *everything*."

I couldn't stand the pain she was in and stupidly tried to explain that the sun wouldn't burn out for a very long time—long after she and her children and even her grandchildren's grandchildren were dead and gone. I'd meant this to be reassuring, but all this talk of death only upset her more. "Stop talking, Daddy," she'd said, covering her ears with her hands the way she used to do when she was four or five. So I stopped, helpless in the face of her burgeoning grief.

Now, Allie pulled the covers up over her head and made herself into a wriggly lump under the pink blanket. "Do I *have* to go to school today?" she asked.

She'd said this with such refreshing and surprising humor, I was glad to play along. "No, but if you don't go to school, you'll have to stay in bed all day long."

She brought her head out from under the covers. "What if I need to pee?"

"You can pee tomorrow."

Allie flung the covers aside and did a slow roll out of bed. "I have to pee *now*."

"Get dressed," I said, giving her a swat on the butt. "While I start the french toast."

The french toast held a certain significance. Before Claire died, I'd made it only on Sundays. A special treat. Now, I made it every weekday morning in a lame attempt to make each day seem special. On Sundays, I took Allie to the local Einstein's, where she ordered something different every time. On our last trip, she'd ordered a plain bagel, toasted, with butter and capers, no lox. No cream cheese. She claimed it was delicious but said so with such a blank face and narrowed eyes I couldn't tell if she meant it or was pulling my leg.

It wasn't only at Einstein's that Allie was intent on change. One time, she wanted her hot chocolate with marshmallows, the next with little cinnamon hearts, and then with tiny pieces of cut up Tootsie Roll; each time something new. It was hard to watch, these meaningless little changes, this senseless variety. I felt it had to do with her grief—distracting herself from it with one new thing after another.

At first, I'd tried to keep Claire's memory alive by talking about her. "Claire would be so proud of you, Sweetpea. All A's and B's this time." Or, "Your mother loved the way you look in that dress. You know that, right?" But whenever I mentioned Claire, Allie would become mute and withdraw into herself. Once, while Allie was on the sofa reading a magazine, I'd sat next to her. "You don't like to talk about Mom?" I'd asked. Allie shook her head and I could tell she was holding back tears. "It makes me sad to talk about her, too," I said. "But I'm even sadder when we don't. Know what I mean?"

"*No,*" she said, quickly and with surprising anger. "It makes me sadder when we *do* talk about her."

I gave her a moment. "But don't we have to talk about her sometime?"

"Not today." Allie said this as though issuing a command.

"You'll let me know when you're ready?"

Allie nodded almost imperceptibly, then picked up her magazine and resumed reading.

• • •

In the kitchen, bright with light flooding through a trio of high windows, I gathered eggs and milk from the refrigerator, started the electric griddle and opened a new loaf of bread. True to her penchant for post-Claire variety, Allie liked to experiment with different kinds of bread for her french toast. This morning it would be sourdough. I broke eggs and mixed them with milk and cinnamon and dunked two pieces of bread in the eggy mixture, feeling happy to do so. Making breakfast for Allie was a way to make a little bit of difference in her life, hopefully for the better. As I set the sodden bread on the griddle, Allie walked into the adjoining room and threw her backpack on the table. She was dressed neatly in blue jeans and a light blue shirt that matched the highlights in the darker blue of her eyes. Her blonde hair, which just reached her shoulders, was expertly parted in the middle. "I'm ready," she announced.

I was smitten and let her know it with a smile. But I was also sad for Allie. Before the accident, Claire had helped her dress every morning. I'd observed the ritual often enough to know it had been an intimate time—Claire picking out a pair of blouses or slacks or shoes for Allie to choose from, holding them up against her own tall, thin frame. Letting Allie know how pretty she was. How could Allie not miss those girly, chatty, irreplaceable moments? I certainly did.

When the french toast was ready—light brown on top and bottom with the sweet, peppery scent of cinnamon—I put it on a plate I'd warmed in the oven and took it out to her along with my own bowl of cereal. She didn't thank me, which was okay; I liked that she took my care for granted. I sat across from her, watching her type something into her phone between bites of french toast. The phone was new; I'd splurged for it on her ninth birthday two months before. Claire would not have approved; she'd have thought Allie too young for a cellphone. But Allie had been delighted and I didn't regret the purchase.

As she was finishing the last few bites of toast, Allie's forehead wrinkled and a dark veil of worry came into her eyes. "I wish I didn't know about the sun dying," she said, looking at me with an expression so forlorn I felt a rush of irritation toward the older girl who'd presented her with this unnecessary bit of knowledge. "It makes things seem...*pointless*. You know?"

I could think of nothing to say to take her mind off this worry. After a minute or so, I asked how she liked the sourdough.

"It's pretty good," she said, raising a final forkful and cocking her head to one side, appraising it. "I still like the rosemary best." Rosemary focassia the week before. Allie popped the spongy bread into her mouth and swallowed without chewing. Then her voice took on a note of urgency. "Can we get the kitten after school today?"

Her best friend, Liz, had offered a kitten and I wasn't about to say no. It was good to see Allie look forward to something. "Sure, Sweetpea," I said. "Unless you think getting the kitten would be… pointless." I immediately wanted to take back what I'd said. I was a psychotherapist, for God's sake. I would never dismiss a patient's worry like this, or try to talk her out of it. Never ever. Of course, Allie wasn't a patient, and a nine-year-old girl shouldn't be worried about something that wouldn't happen for, what—tens of millions of years? Or was it hundreds of millions? I made a note to look it up.

Allie straightened in her chair and looked me in the eye. She spoke as though to a small child, for whom obvious things need to be carefully spelled out. "If the sun's gonna burn out one day and everything in the whole wide world—the entire *universe*—will be destroyed…don't you think we should care about that?"

I was tempted to correct her about the universe. It was only our solar system, not the "entire universe" that would be destroyed. But our solar system, our little planet, *was* her entire universe. And mine. "You do worry about it, don't you?" I said.

"I don't understand why you *don't*." Then, a bit louder, "Why do we keep acting like nothing has happened?"

I was confused. Was Allie finally talking about her mother's death? But she said nothing more, just continued to stare as if disbelieving I could be so dense. I decided to take a chance. "You're right, Allie. It *is* crazy for us to go about our lives as if nothing happened."

I was tired of not talking about Claire; maybe Allie was, too.

A flicker of hurt passed through Allie's face and then was gone as she wiped her mouth with a napkin. "Come on, Daddy," she said. "We'll be late for school."

I wondered if I should tell her it was Claire's birthday. Did she even know? Maybe if I said something, a door would open. But it might just as easily upset her, and it was past time for us to leave for school. I decided I would bring it up that afternoon.

I dropped Allie off at school and drove toward my psychotherapy practice in Miami Shores, not far from where Allie and I lived. As I drove, I wished Claire were there to talk with about Allie's worry regarding the sun. Claire often knew how to reach Allie when I could not. I was sure Claire would tell me it was perfectly natural for Allie to worry, that what she needed wasn't for me to distract her or chide her but to worry *with* her. Just because it wouldn't affect us in our lifetimes didn't mean it wasn't important. "We're all in this together," I could almost hear Claire say. "That's what Allie is thinking. Isn't that a good thing?"

It was a good thing. I relaxed then, grateful for the nearness of Claire's presence. My mind turned to something else I wanted to talk with Claire about: the two things she'd said moments before the accident that took her life.

"I can't do this anymore."

Then, "I'm seeing someone."

They say the spouse always knows. I had a friend once whose wife was cheating on him, and he said that after his wife told him about her affair, things that hadn't made sense before fell into place like cars of a freight train barreling right out of town. Betty had started exercising, was dressing better, looking better. She claimed to have made new friends at the gym and now spent some Friday evenings out with them. Late. Of course, it turned out there never were any "gym friends." Just one special friend.

A week or two before the accident, I'd asked Claire if she was happy. She hadn't said anything, only stared at me in the vacant way she often did when I tried to reach beneath her surface—a stare that fended me off not by looking away, but by looking relentlessly *at* me. This time I'd been determined to hold eye contact until she said something, but after one or two impossibly long minutes, I looked away.

I now regretted looking away. If I'd pressured Claire into speaking what was on her mind *then* instead of when we were both in the car, maybe she'd still be alive.

I couldn't think about that; it was too painful, and unproductive. I turned my attention to the day ahead and its demanding schedule of patient appointments. I liked immersing myself in patients' lives, drawing out surprising and unknown aspects of their stories. I liked helping them see themselves differently. I was scheduled to see a new patient toward the end of the day. This would give me a new world to step into, a welcome distraction from my own fractured existence.

What was her name? Angela something. She'd sounded young, and Latino.

And scared.

CHAPTER TWO

Angela Morales sat up in bed after having had sex with Ricardo Raphael, who was sleeping beside her. *Nice and quick this time,* she thought, pleased with how efficient she'd become at dispatching his desires. Now she was alone again, alone with her thoughts. She drew her knees up to her chin and looked out the condo's floor-to-ceiling window. The blue ribbon of Florida's Intracoastal Waterway wove through a seemingly endless series of luxurious condominium buildings, reminding her how beautiful the world could be. *Just like sex,* she thought. *The world's beauty beckons and allures, but it cannot touch the loneliness I feel inside.*

Across Biscayne Bay, beyond the wide strip of buildings of Miami Beach, she could see the gently rolling swells of the Atlantic Ocean. She imagined swimming there, in the pale blue water, swimming free of Ricardo. Finally, free. The thought made her smile. She was an excellent swimmer, after all; the one good thing she'd taken from her childhood. When she turned from the window, Ricardo had awakened and was looking at her in that way he had of seeming to possess her, his black eyes enveloping her. She felt cold, suddenly, and wrapped a pillow around her stomach. She remembered a time when she'd craved that look, would have given anything to have it. No more. She retrieved her cellphone from the bedside table and began a game of free cell solitaire. Ricardo's flight to Colombia wasn't for another couple of hours, but she wished he would go ahead and *vamoose.*

"Angie," Ricardo said, his voice gravelly and annoyed.

"Yeah?" She didn't look up from the phone, hoping he would give up trying to talk. But he never gave up anything easily.

"Put the fucking phone down, will you?" Angela lay the phone in the nest of silken hair between her thighs and turned toward him. "Is something wrong?" Ricardo asked.

"No," she lied. She couldn't tell him she'd decided to leave. She'd been thinking about it for a long time but just moments before, looking into the endless water, she'd made the decision. *I'm a good swimmer,* she reminded herself. But what a ruckus her leaving would cause. She thought about that word, "ruckus." She'd learned it only the day before, listening to a talk show. She liked that it sounded just like what it meant.

"You can't wait until I'm gone to play with the cards on your phone?" Ricardo was still annoyed.

"I've got a lot on my mind." *If only you knew.*

"Such as?"

"I don't know."

He sat upright in the bed and leaned back against the headboard. "C'mon Angie. I'm in no mood for the games. What is it? You need money?"

She rolled her eyes. With Ricardo, it was always about money.

"What, then?"

She looked down at the black satin sheets with slices of watermelon pictured at odd angles. "I don't want to do this anymore," she said, surprising herself. She hadn't meant to tell him until she'd gotten more prepared. On the other hand, now was as good a time as any. Better than most, actually, since he'd be leaving town soon.

"You don't want to do what anymore—sex before breakfast?" A big smile on his face. He put his hands behind his head, elbows spread wide, grinning at her.

"I mean our 'arrangement,'" she said, putting air quotes around the word, "arrangement." She could hear the cold in her voice.

He gave her a dismissive look. "We don't have an *arrangement,* Angie. We have a *life*."

She couldn't believe how dense the man was, how self-centered. She sat up cross-legged in the bed. "*You,*" she said, far more passionate now than when they'd been having sex. "*You* have a life. Me, not so much."

He took his hands from under his head and grunted. "Most women would kill to have the life you have." He paused, studying her with his eyes. "Have you forgotten what your life was like before?"

She looked away. Of course she hadn't forgotten. Hadn't forgotten going to bed hungry night after night, or waking up to find her mother passed out on the couch, or fending off one or another of her mother's boyfriends, not always successfully. This last part Ricardo didn't know about, only how poor she'd been and the kind of woman her mother was. But maybe he'd guessed the rest.

"You can't quit me, Angie." Ricardo's voice was gentle now. "You know that."

"I got a *job*," she said, looking at him again. She'd expected this news to startle him, but he smiled patiently, as though humoring a child. She made a wide circle with her hands to indicate everything around her. "This place is paid for. So what I make at the bank will be enough, you know? Enough for me to live on. *By myself.*" Ricardo had purchased the condo twenty-five years before, when he'd opened the Miami office of his Colombian law firm. Nearly a year ago, on her twenty-first birthday, he'd put the condo in her name. This had surprised her, and for weeks after she'd felt truly grateful. Gradually, though, she realized he acted like it was still his, and she wondered if he'd had another motive to put it in her name—something financial she didn't know about and couldn't understand.

"Angela," he said, still unperturbed, "If you want a job at a bank, I can get you a job with a bank downtown, and for probably twice what you could make on your own." He placed a hand on her leg, then moved slowly from knee to groin as he leaned into her. "You are not some *chica* I can replace like a car or a boat. You are a part of my life now. As much as Evy and the kids."

She took his hand from between her legs. She wanted to slap him with it, but instead simply laid it on the bed. Not for a minute did she believe she was as important to him as his wife and children in Colombia. "If you really care about me," she said, "you will want what is best for me. *No?*"

He elbowed his way up into a sitting position and then rose from the bed. "Cut the bullshit, Angie. Caring about you means I want you in my life."

She spoke to his back as he picked up the socks he'd left on the floor earlier. "You've been good to me, you have," she said, "but you need someone younger now, like I was when we started." She'd been sixteen when he'd taken her in. Only five years ago, but it seemed like forever.

Ricardo slipped his foot into one of the silk socks. Though remarkably fit for a man in his fifties, he looked silly as he lifted the other foot high and bent over to put a sock on it, his flaccid penis jiggling like a burst balloon. "I'm not discussing this," he said. She watched as he pulled on a pair of boxer-briefs, then took a navy-blue shirt with thin charcoal stripes from a hanger in the closet and a pair of black slacks. He tossed the slacks on the bed and started to put on the shirt. "You know who I work for," he said. "The sort of people they are. *What they do.*" He caught her eye and held her gaze as he buttoned the shirt. "Quitting me is not an option. Do you understand this?"

"I understand, Ricardo." She stretched out on the bed again, turning her face to the wall as a dense ball of dread formed in her gut. She tried to focus on the wall, the utter whiteness of it, and not on Ricardo's implied threat. Would he really hurt her, or have her hurt? Yes, if he was pushed too far. She had no doubt he would. She'd seen it happen with other people who'd crossed him. She heard him zip his suitcase closed and walk out of the bedroom. After a moment more, the front door to the condo slammed shut.

Tension drained from her stomach. She took a deep breath and tried to imagine herself once more in the ocean, swimming free. This time the image wouldn't hold. She kept coming back to Ricardo, his voice saying, "Quitting me is not an option." She could almost hear her mother calling her a *chica tonta,* a silly girl, for wanting to give up everything Ricardo could provide in order to take an entry-level job as a bank clerk. Maybe her mother was right. Maybe, after she was on her own, she would miss everything she took for granted now. But she didn't like the way Ricardo made her feel. *Belittled.* She spoke the word out loud, into the empty room. She'd learned the word a month ago, when she'd been looking through a Spanish-English dictionary, trying to find a way to express in English what it was like to be around Ricardo. Belittled. Made to feel small. Unimportant.

She turned from the wall and reached for a book on the bedside table. She retrieved from within its pages the slip of paper upon which she'd written the name of the psychotherapist with whom she'd made an appointment for later that day.

Dr. Paul Mason, LMHC.

CHAPTER THREE

I had no receptionist, just a small waiting room with a little bell patients could tap to indicate their arrival, and a sign indicating I would come out for them at their appointed time. It was four o'clock, time to meet the new patient I'd been looking forward to. Angela. When I opened the door, the woman sitting there was unusually beautiful: lithe and long-limbed with waist length ink-black hair and skin the color of creamed coffee. She looked up from a magazine she'd been reading and I was startled by the color of her eyes: an impossibly pale blue, the color of the water where the Caribbean Sea meets the shore. They pulled me toward her as a drowning person might reach for the outstretched hand of someone come to help.

"Hello," I said, with genuine warmth, "I'm Dr. Mason. You can call me Paul."

• • •

Angela was intrigued by the doctor's demeanor. The look that passed between them had been intimate but no come-on. Unlike most men meeting her for the first time, he hadn't been "checking her out." It was more like he'd been trying to *see* her, who she really was.

She introduced herself and followed the doctor into his office. There were three chairs to choose from, all of them identical, nicely cushioned, light grey in color. She chose the one closest to the doctor, where she sat to his left at a forty-five-degree angle. She studied him as he settled into his own high-backed leather chair. He was handsome, somewhere north of forty, with rounded shoulders and a softly featured face.

She had no idea how to begin. Several times, while waiting for her appointed time, she'd nearly stood up and left. The idea of breaking off with Ricardo was appealing, but to actually *do* it—she didn't see how she could.

"What brings you here?" the doctor asked. A simple question. But how to answer it? Should she begin by saying she wanted to leave Ricardo and why, or by explaining how she'd come to know Ricardo in the first place? And then how to talk about the real problem: the emptiness inside? She looked down at her feet and noticed her red toenails protruding through the open spaces of her sandals. She thought how Ricardo liked to wrap his strong hands around the arches of her feet and massage them, something she enjoyed still. She became aware she was shaking her head slightly, as though making a small "no, no" gesture. She looked again at the doctor. His grey-blue eyes gave nothing away.

"Help me out here," she said. "I've never done this before." She had thought the doctor would lead her in a series of structured questions, intelligently designed to reveal her problem.

"Well, what prompted you to call me?" he asked.

She had to look away from his penetrating eyes. "I couldn't stop shaking."

She remembered this moment well. It had been two days ago, right after she'd been hired at the bank. Getting the job had given her a shot of courage and she'd decided to make this appointment, something she'd been thinking about for a long time. With a job, she could afford it without Ricardo knowing. She'd gotten the doctor's name from a friend at the gym where she worked out. Thinking about calling him had been okay, but when she'd actually picked up the phone, her hands shook. In a way this had let her know she was doing the right thing. She needed help to leave Ricardo. She couldn't do it on her own.

The doctor was looking at her intently. A kind smile appeared on his face and in his eyes. "What was shaking you?" he asked, and before she could think of what to say, his expression shifted slightly, as though he'd thought of something. "Or who?"

For a moment it was like he *knew* her, knew why she was here. "A man," she said. "He stays with me when he's in Miami. He..." She felt herself flush and wondered if the doctor could see it in her face, on her neck. "He...supports me."

"Tell me about him," the doctor asked, surely unaware of what he was asking. Ricardo was no ordinary man.

It was silly to think Ricardo might be able to hear her, but she couldn't help lowering her voice. "He is an important man. A powerful man. In Colombia especially, but here, too." She looked away again. Where two walls of the office joined there was a spot in which the paint formed a little ridge. It shouldn't be there, this tiny lump of plaster and paint. The doctor should have fixed it. "This man," she said, looking at the doctor again, her voice wavering. "I want to leave him." Her stomach clenched, released, clenched again. She shut her eyes and kept them closed for what seemed like a long time. When she opened them again, the doctor was leaning forward in his chair.

"What is it like," he asked, "to think of leaving?"

She held the doctor's eyes with hers for many moments and was surprised to find that his grey eyes, so calm, calmed her as well. "If I leave him," she said, "there could be trouble. And besides, I'm not sure I even know who I am apart from him."

The doctor's face took on a look of concern. "You said there could be trouble. Are you in physical danger?"

Angela willed her mouth to stay shut. Whatever made her think she could talk about Ricardo? It was not possible to talk about him, what he did for a living. What he might do to her.

Again, there was kindness on the doctor's face. "You don't want to say what the danger is because you don't know? Or because you don't want to tell me about it?"

To answer him at all she would have to reveal too much. She expected the doctor to press her, but instead he asked, "Can you tell me how you and this man met?"

There would be no harm in that. "I'll call him Roberto," she said. "That's not his real name." The doctor nodded, not questioning her choice to conceal Ricardo's identity. Then she told him how a friend of hers, Eric, had been busted for selling cocaine. The cops had wanted Eric to give up his supplier, but he refused. After Eric got out on bail, the supplier referred Eric to Roberto. "Roberto's a lawyer downtown," Angela told the doctor. "Eric asked me to come with him to his appointment—you know, for support. When he came out of Roberto's office, Eric introduced me to him. Roberto surprised me by asking for my number. I didn't understand. I was only sixteen. Of course I didn't let Roberto know how young I was. The next day, he called and asked me out." Angela laughed, remembering. "We went to dinner and to a concert. Of course, I didn't care for the concert but I was *thrilled* to have the attention of such an important man. The next weekend he took me to Bimini on his yacht. *Bimini.* I couldn't believe it. It was like a dream, you know?" Angela took a deep breath, embarrassed by what she had to say next. "In time, I found out he was married, with twin girls in Colombia who were very young." Unexpected tears came to her eyes and the doctor handed her a tissue. She wondered what he thought of her now, the mistress of a married man.

"Do you think this man cares about you?" the doctor asked.

Angela wiped her tears away, held the damp tissue in her hand as she spoke. "At first I thought he cared about me, and then for a long time I didn't. But when he paid off my mother's house…he didn't have to do that." Remembering this gesture, she felt grateful to Ricardo all over again.

"So your mother knows about your relationship with Roberto."

"Yes. She's jealous about it. 'A hell of a lot better than cleaning other people's houses,' is what she said."

The doctor sat back in his chair, crossed his legs. "That's what your mother does? Cleans houses?"

"Yes."

"What was your relationship with your mother like before you met Roberto?"

Angela had expected this question, or one like it. Still, it wasn't easy to talk about her mother. "She had a boyfriend, Brian. He…" She looked away, a taste of bile in her throat, "He did stuff."

The doctor's voice was soft. "You mean sexually? To you."

She still could not look at him. "Yes."

"Did your mother know?"

She looked at the doctor again and was touched by the care evident in his eyes and on his face. "I told her to keep him *off* me." She remembered the anger she'd felt at the time, feeling it anew. "But she said it was my *fault*. That I was trying to steal her man. After that, when Brian knew he could get away with stuff…"

A movie unreeled in Angela's mind: Brian's sweaty chest covering her face as he pushed into her, both hands laced around the top of her head. She could feel his penis inside her as she remembered this, and her mind did now what it had done then: it took her to Pietra, her grandmother, the two of them rocking side by side on the covered porch of Pietra's small house in Venezuela, her grandmother smiling at her from beneath the wide brim of her straw hat, her brown eyes set within a face so old and wrinkled Angela thought it might well be the face of God.

"Angela?"

It was the doctor, asking her to come back. She didn't want to. She wanted to stay where she was, in Venezuela. Where she was safe. She looked up and couldn't remember what she'd been talking about.

"Where did you go just now?" the doctor asked.

She looked into his grey eyes without speaking. She didn't want to take him to Venezuela. Didn't want to talk about Pietra. He seemed to understand, because after a moment he asked, "So how did the business with Brian come to an end?"

She could feel the wooden handle of the knife in her hand. She spoke as if in a trance. "When I was thirteen, I got hold of a kitchen knife and told him, 'If you ever do that again, I'll cut your dick off. *In your sleep*.'"

Angela couldn't believe the doctor was laughing at her. For a long time, neither of them spoke.

"What is it like for you to tell me this, Angela?" the doctor asked.

She looked away, to a window across the room. The blinds were shut, but the top two slats were missing and she could see the sky outside. A light rain was falling. "It's okay," she lied.

"Something happened between us," the doctor said. "You became very quiet. Can you tell me what you were thinking?"

She told herself she could walk out as easily as she'd walked in. "You were laughing at me."

"You mean after you told me you threatened to cut off Brian's penis?"

"Yes."

"I wasn't laughing at you, Angela. I smiled because I liked the way you got yourself out of the hell Brian put you through. I thought it was very smart. And brave."

She studied the doctor. It looked like he was telling the truth. Another spell of silence fell between them, but this time it was okay. Then the doctor asked, "What was it like when your mother blamed you for Brian raping you?"

Her mother's face came to mind, the hard angles of her cheeks and chin. Tears began to rise, but she stopped them before the doctor could see them.

"I tried so *hard* with her, you know?"

"How so?"

"I tried to make her happy. I wanted her to love me, you know? But after she didn't believe me about Brian, I didn't care anymore." She looked out the top of the window again, where trees were bending in the wind. "The thing is, she didn't even notice."

"She didn't notice you'd quit trying?"

"That's right." She looked at the doctor again. "She sure notices me now, though."

The doctor scrunched his nose up in a way he hadn't done before. "Maybe it's Roberto's money she sees?"

She shrugged. He got it.

"What about your father?" he asked. "Where is he?"

Angela felt her stomach drop. "I don't know where he is."

The doctor looked at her like he knew there was more to tell, and he was asking with his eyes for her to tell it. She felt pain deep in her groin and involuntarily closed her own eyes. "I didn't come here to talk about him."

After some time, the doctor spoke again. "Any siblings?"

Angela allowed herself to look at the doctor. She shook her head. "Just me."

The doctor waited a moment, then cleared his throat. "You said earlier, you don't have a sense of who you are apart from Roberto."

That he remembered this was—what's the word? Astonishing. And really, it's why she'd come.

"Tell me what you mean by that."

When she looked down to think of what to say, Angela noticed the doctor was wearing green socks with black pants and his shoes were brown. Had she made a mistake, coming here? Trusting a man who couldn't even dress properly? She looked again at the little clump of plaster and paint where the walls came together, then back at the doctor. It was the kindness in his eyes that convinced her to continue. "When I think about leaving Roberto," she said, "I feel excited at first, but then I get an empty feeling, like if you took all the stuffing out of a teddy bear."

"So, you're Roberto's teddy bear?" A slight smile creased the doctor's face.

"More like an X-rated teddy bear," she said, smiling now too. "Actually, what I mean is, he's *my* teddy bear."

"Do you mean Roberto has become a part of you, a part of the *'stuff'* inside you, and who would you be without that? Without him?"

That was exactly what she meant.

"So why do you want to leave, then?"

"I met someone else." Michael's face came to mind. His chiseled cheeks, black hair, light brown eyes. The respect he showed her. "Someone I could have a *real* relationship with. You know?"

"Tell me more about what you mean by 'real.'"

"With Roberto, it's like I belong to him."

"And with Michael?"

She sat up straighter in the chair. "He believes in me. He makes me think I could be something different than what I am."

"How do you mean?'"

"I know I'm important to Roberto, but it's really all about him. With Michael, it's about me, too." She paused, not knowing how to put the next part. "Sometimes, I think if I leave Roberto for Michael, I'll just be trading one man for another."

"An excellent point." The doctor appeared to think a moment before speaking again. "Were you happy with your life with Roberto before you met Michael?"

"There were some good things, but it got to where I didn't want him to come back from Colombia. He goes there regular. He noticed I wasn't so happy when he returned and he thought I was depressed. He made me see a psychiatrist. The psychiatrist gave me some drug... started with a 'Z'...and I took it for a while, but Roberto didn't like it because it killed my sex drive. He told me, 'If you don't stop taking those damn pills, *I'm* going to get depressed.'" She laughed, and the doctor laughed, too. Then she told the doctor she'd adopted a practice of using the time Roberto was in Colombia to improve her life. She'd earned a GED and now had nearly enough credits for an AA degree from Miami-Dade College.

"Congratulations," the doctor said, his face bright. Then he put his hands together as if in prayer. "I'm thinking about your worry you might be trading one man for another. That might be the case, but sometimes a new relationship can open up possibilities we never imagined. Possibilities to become different ourselves. It sounds like this might be the case with Michael."

The doctor had just put into words something she'd felt but didn't quite know how to say. "So maybe I won't just be trading one man for another?"

"It depends on how you do it. It sounds like the two relationships offer you two very different options for your life. Perhaps with Michael, you can take your time. Find out more about who you are. Who you are with him. And who you want to become."

She felt excited and let it show. "Did I tell you I got a job? A real job?"

The doctor smiled. "No, you didn't." He seemed pleased about this, and she felt a little thrill to have pleased him. "Tell me about it."

"I'll be a teller at a bank. Right here in the Shores. I'm excited, but...I wonder if I'll stick with it. Roberto takes care of me in a way I could never afford on my own."

"What does your excitement tell you?" the doctor asked.

"That I *want* to stick with it?"

He smiled again, this time where she could see his teeth. "It's almost the end of the hour," he said, "but I have one more question."

She waited for it.

"Have you ever had any recurring dreams? Dreams that you have over and over again?"

It was a strange question, but there was a dream like that and she didn't mind telling him about it. "My mother and I flew from Venezuela to America when I was eleven. In the dream I'm on that airplane. I'm in the window seat, looking out at the sky, trying to see the ground below us, to see Venezuela for the last time. All I can see is an unending blanket of clouds."

The doctor's voice was hushed. "What is that like?"

"I want to go back. Venezuela was my home." She remembered what her mother had said when they left, that she would never be able to see Pietra again. Tears came to her eyes and this time she let the doctor see them. "In the dream, I want to go back and see Pietra, my grandmother. I look over at Mother. Her eyes are closed and for some reason I think she might be dead. I wonder who will take care of me now. Alone on this airplane going to a country I do not know." A fraction of the panic from the dream was with her now.

The doctor leaned forward, his voice still soft. "Is that what you wonder, too, when you think about leaving Roberto? Who will take care of you if you do that?"

An electric feeling ran through her. The doctor had just shown her something she didn't know was there, something important. A connection. But she wasn't ready to let him know he was right. It was too private.

The doctor sat back in his chair. "We're at the end of our time for today," he said. "Next time, I'd like to hear more about Pietra."

They made an appointment to meet again in four days—Monday of the following week.

• • •

I was pleased—it had been a good beginning with an exceptionally promising patient. I walked over and opened the blinds of my office window and looked toward the golf course across the street. The rain had stopped and a foursome stood on the 14th tee. I knew the hole well. It was virtually impossible to drive the ball long enough to get past the dogleg that would enable one to reach the green in two. I wondered if the players on the tee knew how futile their hopes were. For some reason, this reminded me of Allie and her worry about earth's doomed future. I hadn't thought about her all session and now, more than anything, I wanted to see her, find out how her day had been.

As I returned to my desk, I noticed a black Mercedes idling along the curb adjacent to the golf course. Inside, two men appeared to be watching Angela as she walked by them on the other side of the street. The driver had a cellphone pressed to his ear. I couldn't be sure, but he seemed agitated as he talked into the phone. With his eyes, he followed Angela closely as she walked past them.

Something Angela had said early in the session came to mind. "*There could be trouble.*"

CHAPTER FOUR

On the way to pick up Allie from her afterschool program, I passed a park she'd named "Allie-fall-down-park" because this was where I'd taught her to ride a bike. In the center of the park is a circular fountain—I could see it now in the distance—and this fleeting glimpse of water sparked a memory I hadn't known was there.

Claire and I had been together about a year. We were hiking and came across a shallow pool of crystal-clear water. Where was it? Colorado? New Mexico? I couldn't remember. There was a rock formation in the center of the pool around which small fish darted, their skin like ribbons of silver lit by the sun. Claire challenged me to catch one of the fish with my bare hands. "I'll bet you *can't*," she said, smiling mischievously. I took off my shoes and stepped into the shallow pool, pretty sure that I could. After all, there were so many of them. I chased the little creatures around and around the tower of rocks, occasionally plunging my hands into the cold water. It was much more difficult than I'd imagined. I was fast, but they were faster. And so very tiny. Just as I was about to give up, I felt something slippery and alive caught in my fingers. Still standing in the pool of water, I offered the little fish, cupped in my hands, to Claire.

"Our little miracle," she'd said, while giving me a look of unfettered love.

I couldn't remember why we'd been out west or for how long. I had no idea what had taken place before this event or after. It was an island memory, lifted from the sea of time, and it caused me to wonder just how the mind decides what to put in its keep-forever box. Had I preserved this particular event because I'd come to experience Claire just as hard to catch as that little fish? Or was it because this had been such a special, unusually light-hearted moment between us?

When I turned into Allie's afterschool program, she was talking with a girl I didn't know. Allie was talking fast, her hands in the air, fingers spread wide. I considered tapping my horn to let her know I'd arrived, but it occurred to me she'd be grown and gone soon enough and I might long for moments like this. Just to watch her. I wondered what she was talking about with such happiness. That she could be so happy, in the midst of our days of grief, seemed a small miracle.

Allie saw my car and quickly ended the conversation. She ran to me and clambered into the car beside me. "Can we get the kitten now?" she asked, buckling her seatbelt.

We hadn't talked about exactly when to pick the kitten up, but I'd thought we might do it right after supper. I'd checked with Liz's mother to see if this time would work for their family. "It's nearly six," I said. "I think we should get something to eat first."

Allie scrunched up her nose. "We can get something to eat after. Then the kitten can eat *with* us." I looked into her eager face and thought this might have been what she'd been talking about with her friend. I knew Allie had been excited to get the kitten, but she seemed especially focused on it now, as though the kitten offered an opportunity to remake her life in some vital way.

"What if Liz is eating supper now?" I said. "We wouldn't want to disturb her."

"Call, Daddy. Find out."

I retrieved my cellphone from the front pocket of my shirt—hers wasn't allowed at school—and handed it to her. "You call."

With great concentration she punched numbers on the phone and put it to her ear. "Lizzy, it's me, Allie. My dad wants to know if you're having supper now, or can we come by and pick up the kitten." These last words came fast, more a declaration than a question. The smile on Allie's face let me know what Liz's answer had been. I had to admit I was excited, too. Having a pet would give us something besides one another to focus on. The family would be three again.

The kitten was calico: white, with irregular patches of cinnamon and black. On the drive home she mewed without ceasing. At one point, she escaped Allie's grasp and scampered across my lap onto the floorboard of the car. I asked Allie to fetch the kitten so it wouldn't interfere with my driving. She unbuckled her seat belt, gathered the kitten up and held it tightly in her lap, keeping it secure with one hand as she re-buckled her seat belt with the other. For a minute or so the kitten howled and struggled against her grasp, but finally it settled and began to purr.

"She's beautiful, isn't she, Daddy?" Allie was stroking her fur.

"Yes, she is. Have you decided what you're going to name her?"

"I'm going to call her 'Onesie.'"

"Onesie?"

"My one and only." She lifted the kitten and brought it to her face, rubbing noses with it. Onesie let out a low moan and stretched her paws to get away.

We drove a while in silence, Onesie falling asleep in Allie's lap. We were almost home when I looked over and saw tears running down Allie's cheeks. I couldn't think what might be wrong. "What's the matter?" I asked.

Allie gathered herself and started stroking the kitten's fur. "I'm gonna miss her *so* much."

"Miss who?"

"Onesie." She looked down at the kitten, still asleep in her lap.

"What do you mean, you're going to miss her?"

"You know, when she dies."

I glanced over at her, confused. "Allie, Onesie won't die for a very long time."

Allie's voice was sharp. "Daddy, we don't know that."

I was mortified. How could I have thought such a thing, said such a thing? Especially today, Claire's birthday. "You're right," I said, "We don't know when Onesie will die. But I hope it won't be for a long, long time."

"Me, too," Allie said this so sincerely, it made me realize how aware she'd become of the fragility of every life. I wished I could relieve her of this tender place in her soul. But I also knew I had been responsible for bringing it about. It was my fault Claire was no longer with us.

After dinner, I watched from the sofa as Allie sat on the carpeted floor and teased Onesie with a piece of string, pulling it across the floor always just out of reach. Once, after Onesie pounced and caught the string, her claws landed on Allie's fingers. "Ouch!" Allie said, drawing her hand away and holding up her injured finger for me to see.

"She didn't mean to," I said, and invited her to join me on the sofa. I took her into my lap and she settled in my arms as we watched Onesie stalk the string as though it were dangerous prey. I felt comforted by Allie's warmth and the small vibrations of her gentle laughter. I didn't want the moment to end. Suddenly, the kitten pounced again and this time jumped straight-legged high into the air. The string, caught on one of the kitten's curved claws, flew up with her. An alarmed Onesie batted furiously at the string as both fell to the ground. The kitten ran off then, as if the string had defeated her.

Through tears of laughter, Allie looked up at me. "Daddy, Onesie makes the string seem *alive*."

"I'm glad we got her," I said, stroking Allie's hair.

"Me, too," she said, and gave me a hug. It was maybe the first time since Claire's death I could imagine life without her. I wasn't ready for such a life yet, but I could imagine it.

Later, after Allie had put on pajamas and gotten into bed, I sat beside her with Onesie stretched out next to us. I was about to kiss her goodnight when I noticed she seemed lost in thought. I thought I might know why. In the pleasure of playing with the cat, I'd completely forgotten it was Claire's birthday. Was that what had come to Allie's mind now? I asked what she was thinking about.

"You know what I learned yesterday? About the sun burning up?"

"I remember." *Not this again.*

"When I asked my teacher about it, he said before that happened the sun would get very big and hot and the earth would be uninhabitable." She looked quickly over at me. "That means no one could live here anymore."

I couldn't help but smile at her playing teacher with me.

"Daddy, does everyone know this?"

"Not everyone," I said. "But many people do. Smart people do." I'd known this basic astronomical fact since I was in middle school, but it had never grabbed me the way it grabbed Allie.

Allie's forehead furrowed. "How come I never heard about it before? I mean, aren't people worried?" She looked up at me and hesitated a fraction before she spoke again. "Are you worried, Daddy?"

I recalled my imaginary conversation with Claire in the car that morning, what I'd learned from it. "When I think about the sun dying," I said, "it does bother me. But I think it's so far in the future, we'll figure something out before it happens."

"But what if we *don't?* What if we can't?" Allie suddenly seemed beside herself with worry. Everything will just be…*gone*." This possibility seemed very real to Allie, as though she might witness it herself. I wished I knew what to say, something that would bring comfort without dismissing her concern. When I failed to speak, Allie shook her head from side to side and asked, her voice breaking, "If the sun's going to die, what does anything matter? *What,* Daddy?"

As I might do with a patient, I tried to think myself into her frame of mind. It was death she was talking about, really. The deaths of those we love. Her mother's death. Our own death to come. In the face of losing everyone and everything, what *does* matter? I asked myself that question. What mattered to me now? Allie watched me with keen interest.

I decided to tell her the simple truth as I knew it. "Here's the thing," I said. "Whenever you and I are together, I feel especially alive." I looked into the depths of her eyes, blue as sapphire. "Know what I mean?" She nodded slowly, getting it. "And this way I feel..." I held up my hands as though weighing an invisible object. "It *matters.* I can't say why, but it does. And it always will. Nothing can change that. Nothing at all."

Allie took this in and then looked down. When she looked up again, I could tell she wanted to ask me something, but was holding back.

I waited.

"Did you feel that way about Mommy?"

My stomach turned. "What way?" Of course I knew what she meant.

"Specially...*alive?*"

"Yes," I said, my voice catching. "I felt that way about your mother."

Allie's voice was small, a raft adrift in a vast ocean. "Me, too." Her face clenched. Tears slipped through the shut lids of her eyes.

Crying myself, I pulled Allie to me and held her until her body settled, then lowered her back onto the bed, where she lay as perfect now as she'd been that morning. I stayed with her until I was sure she was asleep, memories of Claire running through my mind. Our first date, at Starbucks, where we'd lingered nearly two hours feeling each other out. An early trip to South Beach, where we watched the moon rise over the ocean, Claire teaching me about the constellations and how they got their names. The many times we took long walks in the morning before work. I remembered Claire in labor with Allie, how proud I had been. At first, Claire hadn't wanted children. She had dreams of graduate school, a doctorate in mathematics, teaching at the collegiate level. But from the moment Allie was born, Allie had been the most important thing in Claire's life. I was certain she'd had no regrets.

Allie was sleeping now. I rested the palm of my hand on the kitten sprawled beside her. A low rumble emanated from beneath the tiny creature's fur and she lifted her head to look at me. Onesie's eyes narrowed with affection and she placed a paw against my forearm, her touch warm and firm and real.

I felt that finally, with Onesie, Allie and I were moving on in a new way. Moving on beyond Claire.

And then came an unwelcome thought. I wondered if Claire had moved on, too, before she died? Moved on from me? "I can't do this anymore," she'd said. What could that have meant but "I can't do *us* anymore."

"I'm seeing someone." She'd also said that. Had she moved on? How could I have not noticed? Then I realized I might have misunderstood. Maybe she hadn't meant she was having an affair. Maybe she'd meant she was seeing a therapist. "I'm seeing someone." Of course. That's what people say when they are seeing a therapist. And that fit Claire, her style and deliberately contained life, far more than some affair.

"Claire?" I whispered into the darkened room. "Were you?"

Filled with a wonder I hadn't felt before, I rose from the bed and walked to where a picture of Claire rested on an end table in the family room. It seems silly now but I thought somehow the Claire in that picture might be able to tell me what she'd meant. In the photo, she had a slight, enigmatic smile, her blond-brown hair framing eyes more green than blue. A tenderness came over me then, a pure affection undiminished by the way she died and the fact I'd caused it. I touched the glass of her face and spoke the words out loud. "Happy Birthday, Claire."

She would have been forty-one years old. I could imagine her receiving my good wishes and in response came a surprising feeling of gratitude. I was grateful to have had her in my life. I truly was.

Something else I was grateful for, I realized. Something more immediate. Tonight, Allie had opened the door to her grief. Had allowed Claire into our home again, her name to be spoken. For the rest of our lives, I thought, we would be able to share memories and countless stories about Claire.

Like the time I caught a fish with my bare hands. I could hardly wait to share this story with Allie. I didn't think I ever had, since I'd just remembered it myself.

CHAPTER FIVE

The alarm jarred me awake. I'd been dreaming Claire and I were making elaborate preparations for a journey, one in which we'd be gone from home a long time. Right before the alarm went off, she was explaining to me the importance of the trip. The connection between us had been electric.

It took me a moment to realize she wasn't actually there, in bed with me. When I realized this was true, I tried to go back into the dream, desperate to find her again, and that connection between us. Both she and the dream had moved beyond my reach. I tried to remember where Claire and I been preparing to travel in the dream, and why, but I couldn't. I was left with an unsettled feeling, caught between two worlds. Inhabiting neither.

Finally I allowed myself to slip into the present and then remembered how Allie had cried herself to sleep the night before. Was she okay? Still asleep, I hoped. I didn't like the thought she might have awakened alone with her grief. I slipped out of bed and walked quietly down the hallway to her bedroom. She was fast asleep. Did she, too, sometimes dream of Claire. She must. I watched her body slowly rise and fall. She was so much of what mattered to me now. Nearly everything.

I figured I had about an hour before it would be time to wake Allie up, and there was something I badly wanted to do. I went to my study, determined to find evidence Claire had been seeing a psychotherapist before her death. It would be a relief to find out she hadn't been unfaithful. And I thought maybe the therapist could share with me something of Claire's state of mind at the end. I knew confidentiality persists beyond the grave, but maybe I could learn *something.*

After nearly an hour of searching bank records and credit card statements, I could find no payments to someone who might be a therapist. She could have paid cash, of course, or maybe she'd had a whole separate bank account I hadn't known about. More likely, I'd been wrong about her seeing a therapist. In the light of day, I realized this thought had most likely been an attempt to construct a narrative of our life I could stomach more easily than her hooking up with some unknown man, telling lies and keeping secrets, giving me less and less of her real self.

I recalled a telephone call she'd made from a hotel room in Ohio the year before. She and one of her best friends, Valerie, had gone to Ohio to participate in The Great Ohio Bicycle Adventure, a week-long cycling and camping trip across the State. The call was to tell me she and Val had decided to stay over a couple days after the event. "A little vacation," she'd said. I hadn't given much thought to this at the time, though it did occur to me they'd just *had* a little vacation. And there was something eerie about her tone of voice during the call. I wondered at the time if she'd been drinking. Now, I wondered if Valerie had come home and left Claire with someone *else* those extra two days. Was it during this "little vacation" that Claire had begun her affair? Should I ask Val about it now? Could I even trust her to tell me the truth?

Awash in this unwelcome mush of feelings I returned to Allie's bedroom. It was time to awaken her. She must have heard me because she rolled over in bed and drew her pink-pajamaed legs up to her chest. Curled up like that she seemed too small to carry the weight of her mother's death. I knelt next to her and placed my forearms on the mattress of her bed. I whispered her name and watched her blue eyes open and meet mine with a look so ambiguous I couldn't fathom her state of mind. So much like Claire I thought. Hiding in plain sight. When I said good morning, Allie neither responded nor looked away. I held her gaze until she reached out a hand and rested it on my forearm, the same spot where Onesie had placed her paw the night before.

"Where's Onesie?" Allie asked, her voice sleepy.

I hadn't thought about the kitten. I looked around Allie's bed to see if Onesie was there. She wasn't. "I don't know," I said, surprised now I hadn't thought of her before.

Allie pulled her hand away and lifted her head from the pillow. She spoke with a note of disbelief. "You don't know where Onesie is?"

I felt the reprimand and a part of me joined Allie in giving it. "I'll find her," I said.

"You haven't seen her all morning?" This was said as though I'd committed a small crime.

"No, but I'm sure we can find her."

"Daddy, why haven't you looked for her already?" Allie let her head fall back onto the pillow, clearly exasperated.

I looked under the bed, on the other side of the bed, then in the closet where the door had been open. No cat. I left Allie's room and called Onesie's name as I searched through the living room, the dining room, the kitchen, my study. I was beginning to feel frantic when Allie emerged from the hallway with the kitten in her arms, Onesie offering a prolonged yawn, showing her teeth.

"Where was she?" I asked.

"Sleeping on that shelf above your bed. You didn't notice?"

"I guess not."

Allie asked how long I'd been up.

"An hour or so."

She set the kitten on the floor and it scampered toward the kitchen. "You didn't think about Onesie that whole time?"

"I'm sorry, Allie. I was more worried about you." I knelt in front of her so we were face to face. "Remember what we talked about last night, just before you went to sleep?"

Her eyes held a knowing look. "Yes."

I rested my hand on her shoulder, small and bony and warm. "You talked about your mother."

"Yes," she said, a bit defiantly, as though I'd somehow challenged her.

"So, I was worried about you, that's all. It's why I didn't think about Onesie." I took Allie's hand and walked with her into the kitchen, where the kitten circled expectantly, mewing for food. "Let's feed Onesie," I said.

I took a can of cat food from the cupboard, opened it and emptied it into Onesie's bowl. Before I could place the bowl on the floor, Allie said she wanted to "present" the food to the cat. Instead of simply putting the bowl down, she retrieved a fork from a kitchen drawer and carefully shaped the mush of food into a sculpture of a small animal. A mouse, I supposed. "Here you go, Onesie," she said to the desperately yowling kitten. "Eat that." Allie watched with satisfaction as Onesie settled in front of the food and dug in, her little orange head bobbing up and down as she ate.

While Allie dressed, I made french toast, remembering with new regret how I'd never said anything yesterday about it being Claire's birthday. Should I say something now? Maybe we could put together a belated recognition. But I decided to wait, see if she brought it up.

When Allie came to the table, she was wearing her favorite outfit, one she'd picked out herself, a dark blue dress with tiny red hearts along the hemline. I told her she looked great and she performed a little curtsy before sitting down at the table.

"Do you think Mom would have liked Onesie?" she said as we ate.

"How could she not?" I asked, pleased Allie had indeed made a reference to Claire.

"Mom didn't like cats. She called them—not selfish, but something that means the same thing."

"Self-centered?"

"Yeah, that."

I couldn't remember Claire saying anything one way or the other about cats. It struck me that Allie probably knew other things about Claire I didn't know, that the mother she lost was different in many respects from the wife I knew.

After finishing breakfast, I drove Allie to school and headed to my office. It was a Friday and my patient load was light, so I spent the morning catching up on insurance claims. As I entered information into my Electronic Health System, my mind turned to Angela, the new patient I'd seen the day before. I would see her again in just a few days, Monday. I looked forward to it. There was a compelling quality to her story and to her struggle, something compelling about *her,* the way she seemed both innocent and tough at the same time.

I was intrigued, too, by this "Roberto" she wanted to get away from. I remembered she hadn't given his real name and wondered why not. Was he a recognizable figure in the community? I remembered how after the session there'd been that car with men watching Angela leave my office. What a control freak Roberto must be, I thought, having Angela followed like that. And again I remembered Angela's words.

"There could be trouble."

CHAPTER SIX

In my office on Monday, Angela was more at ease—not the scared, deeply troubled young woman I'd met the week before.

"What's on your mind today?" I asked.

Angela said she'd spent the past weekend with Roberto. "I thought, why not have one final weekend together? He had business in Key West and I've always loved it there, so I went along. The night before we came back, I decided to be honest with him. I told him I wanted to try living on my own. He started to get upset but I asked him to just listen for a minute. I told him I was tired of playing second fiddle to his family, of being his showpiece. You know what he told me?" Angela leaned forward, eyes wide, showing me the surprise she must have felt at the time. "He told me *they* were the showpiece. *I* am the one most important. He loves his kids of course but his wife, not so much. Not like he loves me."

I wasn't buying it, but before I could think of what to say, she was talking again.

"He said I didn't understand him. Not really. And then he told me things about himself I never knew. He told me that when he was twelve, his parents and older sister were murdered by the Colombian army." Angela paused to let this sink in.

"Did he tell you how this happened, or why?"

"Roberto's family lived in a village controlled by the FARC—you know, the rebels—and the Colombian army came in and killed everyone, even some of the children. Roberto was spared and taken to an orphanage. Much later, he came to America and got a law degree. Now he works to support the FARC by defending drug dealers because, you know, the cocaine trade is how they get their money. He wants more than anything to avenge his parents' deaths."

I had to admit this story added a layer of complexity to Roberto I hadn't known before. If the story was true, the man wasn't simply self-centered but invested in a larger cause. "So," I said, "Roberto let you into a part of himself you didn't know about. You must see him differently now."

"*Yes.* I didn't know he was committed to anything but himself." Her enthusiasm toward this man she'd so desperately wanted to leave less than a week ago, was striking. I decided to test how far she'd moved in her thinking.

"So now you don't want to leave him?"

"I'm not sure what I want anymore."

"What about Michael?"

She screwed up her face. "I know. I'm in a real…*mess*, aren't I?"

I thought back to the previous session, how eager she'd been to have her own life apart from Roberto, even if she didn't know what that life might look like. "Last time you were here," I said, "I got the impression you didn't much like your life with Roberto. You seemed to feel you had to live on his terms." Angela kept her eyes on mine.

I could tell she was taking in what I'd said, thinking about it. "And now?" I asked.

"I see your point. Even if I'm more important to Roberto than I knew, he still wants to control me."

"Actually, I'm not trying to make a point. I'm trying to understand." Of course, she was right. I did have skin in this game. I couldn't imagine how staying with Roberto could possibly be good for her. I wondered if she knew he'd had her followed to my office last week. I shifted in my chair, crossed one leg over the other. "Angela," I said, "did you notice some men in a black car after our last session?"

"No." She looked genuinely perplexed.

"There was a black car with two Hispanic-looking men inside. They were watching you. One of them was on the phone, and he looked like he was making a report to someone. Might Roberto have been the one he was talking to?"

Worry and alarm took hold in Angela's face.

"Would it be like Roberto to have men follow you, watch you?"

She looked down at her sandals. "Yes, it is like him to do such a thing." Her voice was hollow now, her previous enthusiasm gone.

"Angela—what Roberto told you in Key West, how do you know it's true?"

She seemed to turn this over in her mind. "I don't think the stuff he told me about the way he grew up was a lie. I think that was real. I could tell it in his eyes."

"What about the part about him not loving his wife the way he loves you. Do you think that was true?"

She was quiet for several moments. "I did see them together once. It was at a Christmas party. Evy—that's his wife—flew in from Colombia to be with him."

"And how were they together?"

"She was *beautiful*. So elegant and...sophisticated. I felt like a schoolgirl next to her. Well, I guess I was. And he was different with her. He treated her with respect. More like an equal."

"What was it like for you to see them together?"

"I felt...there's a perfect word for it in English; I learned it later that night, when I looked through my thesaurus. Inconsequential. I felt...inconsequential.'"

I was impressed by her use of such a complex word. "How did you happen to look for that word?"

"Whenever I have a strong feeling, I go to my English thesaurus and find as many words as possible to describe the way I feel. It's a way to, you know, expand my vocabulary."

I pictured her sitting alone in the condo supplied by Roberto, searching through her thesaurus. "Also," I said, "I suppose this exercise distracted you from the pain you were feeling?"

She smiled shyly, so much of her still a girl. "I hadn't thought of that, but I suppose it did. When Roberto and Evy were together, he seemed to truly admire her."

"That must have hurt."

She closed her eyes, took a deep breath, then looked at me again. "It *changed* me, actually. I decided that night to focus on me. *My* life. I enrolled in Miami-Dade College the week after."

I was impressed by the way Angela had used her disappointment with Roberto to take charge of her life. I'd just finished reading a book on "post-traumatic growth." This seemed a good example of it.

For more than a minute we sat in silence, Angela deep in thought. "You're right," she finally said. "I've got to leave him."

I didn't like thinking I'd communicated my private opinion about what she should do. "I'm right?" I asked.

She smiled and flashed her eyes, so pale, yet full of light. "Tell me you don't think so."

I'd been caught, and something seemed to deepen between us, a closer connection. From the beginning of our first session, I'd felt especially drawn to Angela. Why? I wasn't sure, but if I could help her re-claim her life, to own it as she never had before, that would be a fine thing. I looked at the clock and saw it was time to wind the session down. "There's a lot going on," I said. "I think we should meet twice a week for a while—at least until you get things sorted out with Roberto. Can you come in this Thursday?"

"I have a lunch hour every day," she said, adding a note of humor to her voice. "I could come tomorrow."

I knew she was joking, but her eagerness matched the warmth and affection I felt toward her. "Okay," I said. "Let's meet Thursday at twelve."

• • •

I opened the door to my last patient of the day. Like Angela, a new patient. He'd called Friday and asked to come in as soon as I had an opening. The man was large and well-muscled, with thick black hair fashioned into a ponytail and a rather large scar above his right eyebrow. Early fifties, I guessed.

"You are Ricardo?" I asked.

"Yes," the man said, rising from the waiting room chair.

Something about him—the expression on his face, the way he walked—communicated an aura of aggression that made me uneasy. I showed Ricardo into my office and invited him to sit anywhere he liked. Ricardo chose the chair closest to mine and once I took my seat, he leaned in uncomfortably close. I sat back a bit. "What brings you here, Ricardo?" I asked.

The man's voice was brusque, his black eyes narrow but bright. "I want to see what kind of man my Angela talks to."

I couldn't have heard him right. "Excuse me?"

"Angela. Angela Morales. She sees you, correct? She saw you earlier today."

I wouldn't have been more surprised if the man had pulled out a gun and pointed it at me. Nor more alarmed. This must be the mysterious "Roberto." Once I'd regained some semblance of balance, I told him I couldn't reveal the identities of patients I see. "Nor anything they say to me. Surely you know this."

Ricardo laughed. A genuine laugh, without a trace of hostility. "You don't have to 'reveal her identity,' Doctor. I know her identity already. In fact, I know Angela much, much better than you do." Ricardo sat upright. "I make it my business to know about the people in Angela's life. *All* the people in her life." He let the statement sit a moment before continuing. "You, for example. I know you graduated from the University of Texas and then went to the University of Chicago for graduate school." He paused, his eyes never leaving mine. "I know you have a daughter, Allie, and that her fourth-grade teacher is not well-liked. How is she, Dr. Mason? Allie, I mean. How is she managing since her mother's death?"

My world was instantly reduced to the penetrating black eyes of the man sitting across from me, eyes which had just robbed me of any ability to think, or even breathe. *Allie, where is she now?* She should be at home with Sarah, a teacher's aide, doing homework. Ricardo probably knew this. I couldn't take my eyes off him. What did he want? Ricardo was looking at me patiently, undoubtedly aware of the effect he'd had.

I took a breath and tried to sound like a therapist again instead of the terrified father I was. "How can I help you, Ricardo?"

Ricardo leaned too close again, an unmistakably intentional intrusion. "You can answer one question. Is Angela going to leave me?"

"I can't tell you that."

A look of disgust came into Ricardo's face. "But you know this information."

"I can't tell you whether I know it or not." I was beginning to feel in control again. My room, my rules.

"Angela tells you things, yes? About her life, her plans."

"I can't tell you what Angela does or doesn't talk about."

Ricardo looked down. "I know she has talked about me." He looked up again and his lips formed a small smile. "Dr. Mason, I have the ability—or, shall we say, the *resources*—to make you tell me anything I like. *Anything.*"

There was in the man's words a menace so intimate it cleared my mind of everything but the threat itself, the raw violence of it.

"I think we are finished here," Ricardo said. He stood and walked past me and out the door. For many moments I didn't move. Couldn't move. I had no doubt that what Ricardo said at the end was true, that he had ways to make me tell him anything he wanted to know. My mind couldn't help but race through the possibilities: a hammer blow to my knee? An axe to a finger, or worse, my hand? And surely the way he mentioned the specifics of Allie's life was meant as a threat. I felt nauseous, unable to move for a long time. I didn't think I could go to the police, not yet anyway. The threat had been too ambiguous, too expertly vague. I could stop seeing Angela.

That's probably what Ricardo wanted, and it's what my fear would have me do. But my best instincts told me to not let myself be intimidated and controlled by this man, at least not yet. Not until I knew more about the situation I was in.

But what about Allie? Could I put her at risk by continuing to work with Angela? Of course not. Not if Ricardo were truly a danger. But I didn't yet know the man well enough to know whether the threat coming from him was real, or the posturing of a bully.

• • •

In downtown Miami, Angela sat across from Ricardo. She watched as he finished a telephone call, his voice animated, his rough-hewn features broadening into a smile. She remembered how close she'd felt to him only last weekend. She felt foolish now for having been taken in by his Key West story. His past was tragic, yes, but that didn't make the way he treated her okay.

She felt something else, too. Tired of playing the young girl happy to be rescued. With Dr. Paul's help, she'd begun to imagine herself and her life differently.

"Angie, my darling," Ricardo said, putting away the phone and leaning back in his large leather chair. "What brings you to my office?"

She let the venom show. "How *dare* you have people follow me."

The brief look of surprise on Ricardo's face was quickly replaced by a posture of innocent curiosity. "Who told you such a thing?"

"My therapist saw your men watching me when I left his office last week." She wondered if Ricardo would deny it.

He leaned forward, his voice tender. "I should have told you. That way it would not have been a surprise. I had you followed to protect you. I did not know you were going to see a shrink. You should have told me this, no?"

He was trying to shift the blame to her, like always. "Bullshit, Ricardo. Be honest with me, like you were last weekend in Key West."

"Okay, I will tell you the truth. I had you followed because I know about Michael. It is him I thought you were going to see."

He knows about Michael? How in the world had he found out?

"So you see," Ricardo said, "I was relieved to hear you were merely seeing a therapist."

Angela had come into this meeting feeling strong, prepared to confront Ricardo. Now he had turned the tables on her. "What would have happened," she asked, "if I *had* been going to see Michael?" She knew it was a silly question, the question of a scared girl. Silly because Ricardo would never tell her the truth about this. But she had to ask.

"The same as what happened at Dr. Mason's office," Ricardo said. "My men would have reported it to me. Told me where you met, what you did together. That sort of thing."

Angela realized this must have already happened.

Ricardo continued talking. "As long as we're being honest, there is something else you should know." He waited a beat, studied her. "I have met your shrink, Dr. Mason."

Angela felt as though she'd been ripped in two. She didn't try to hide her surprise.

"Yes," Ricardo said. "I met him today. In his office. I wanted to check him out. I believe the word is 'vet.' I wanted to vet him. I do this for you." He folded his hands together on top of his desk.

Did he really believe she would buy that? "You did this for *me?*" she asked, nearly shouting. She couldn't think of anything to say that would adequately express her outrage, so she simply turned and walked out of his office. She got into her car, but before driving back to her condo she took out her phone and punched in the number that would connect her to Michael. She asked him to meet her for dinner the next evening.

He said that he would.

CHAPTER SEVEN

After I pulled into my driveway, I sat in the car a minute to try to settle myself and to think. I was still out of sorts from the session with Ricardo. I kept hearing his threat in my mind, about how he had "resources" to make me tell him anything. The feeling in my stomach told me this threat was real. Yet Angela had fast become one of my favorite patients and I was certain our work together could make an important difference in her life. I didn't know what to do. I could neither imagine terminating my work with her—there was nothing she'd done to justify such an action—nor could I imagine continuing it. My mind ping-ponged back and forth between these two options with such rapidity it made me dizzy. I decided I would just have to wait and collect more information.

On the two nights I worked late, Sarah, the teacher's aide, walked Allie home from school and helped her with homework until I arrived. I opened the door expecting to see Allie and Sarah on the floor of the family room, working with the TV on in the background. But the room was empty, the television dark, the entire house so quiet I could hear the soft tick of the clock on the family room wall. I walked into the kitchen, not really surprised to see no one there either. It was too quiet. I searched my study, Allie's bedroom, my bedroom, repeatedly calling out for Allie and Sarah. Even the garage was empty. With an escalating worry, I went to my study and sat in the leather chair in front of my desk trying to think what to do. Surely Ricardo hadn't done something to Allie. Too soon for that. Wasn't it? Onesie startled me by jumping onto the desk. I hadn't notice her when I searched the house. The kitten paraded back and forth in front of the computer monitor, meowing for attention. I absent-mindedly rubbed her fur while with my other hand I retrieved my cellphone from my pants pocket to call Sarah. I'd turned the phone off so as not to disturb my therapy sessions; now I pushed the right buttons and waited for it to open. When it did, there were two messages on its reflective surface: *Sarah Meyners Missed Call* and *Sarah Meyners Voicemail.* I played the voicemail.

"Paul, this is Sarah. Allie really, *really* wanted to go down to the bay. If we're not home when you get there, that's where we'll be." Relief washed through me even as I wondered why. Why had they gone to the bay?

Biscayne Bay, only four blocks from the house. It's where Allie used to go with her mother nearly every day after school. There were ducks to feed, and Claire liked to be near the water, liked the rhythm of it moving against the land, liked the open space between Miami Shores and Miami Beach. "Room to breathe," she'd often said. "At the bay, there's room to breathe."

So far as I knew, Allie hadn't been there since Claire died. Something must have called her to the water. Was it because she'd allowed Claire to live in her mind and heart again? I got in my car and forgot about the speed limit. A block from the bay, I made a guess and turned left. After another block I saw Sarah sitting on a bench by the bay. I followed her gaze to Allie, who was throwing bits of bread into the water. Ducks and fish competed for the doughy prizes.

It was good to see Allie. Even though I didn't know whether or not Ricardo's implied threat to Allie was real, I'd been truly scared when she hadn't been at home. Here she was, safe and sound. I parked, got out of the car and walked toward her. She didn't turn to greet me as I approached. That was odd. I sat beside her on the grass and spoke her name but still she didn't respond. What in the world could be going on? She tore off a small square of bread and threw it into the bay. Three large ducks thrashed the water, fighting for the food. Not looking at me, she said, in a scolding voice, "You forgot Mommy's birthday last week."

I felt as guilty as if I *had* forgotten. "I didn't forget," I said. "I just didn't say anything about it." This sounded both lame and unlikely. I didn't expect her to believe it. "Did you want to do something special for Mommy's birthday?" I asked.

She finally turned to me. "No, I didn't remember Mommy's birthday either. I only thought about it today. At school." Her face took on the look of a teacher admonishing a student for bad behavior. "You shouldn't lie about it, Daddy."

"Lie about what?"

"About forgetting."

"Allie, honest, I didn't forget. I didn't say anything last week because I didn't want to upset you."

She looked at me as though I didn't get her at all. "I hate it when you treat me like a baby," she said, angrily.

Her anger was hard to take. "I'm sorry," I said. And I was. I looked at her, willing her to soften her stance, but she didn't. "Maybe we could do something tonight for Mommy's birthday. Would you like that?" She turned and looked across the choppy water, her expression unreadable. I waited a moment or two before adding, "What would you like to do, Allie?"

"A cake," she said, still looking beyond the water. "With candles. Red ones for each year she was alive and a blue one for the part of the year she's been gone."

The simple elegance of her plan caused my throat to clench. I asked what kind of cake she wanted.

"Chocolate fudge brownie."

Of course. Claire's favorite. "Okay," I said. "We'll drop Sarah off, then go by the grocery store and get some stuff for dinner and the makings for a chocolate fudge brownie cake."

"And one other thing," she said, her voice still prickly cold.

"Yes?"

"Can we put a picture of Mom on the table?" It wasn't really a question.

I didn't want a picture of Claire on the table. I didn't want to relive the horror of her death, nor the sickness of knowing I'd caused it. But I couldn't say no.

• • •

Allie and I sat across from one other at the dining room table, a large picture of Claire positioned in front of an empty chair where she used to sit. The picture had been taken on her fortieth birthday. Her last. She was looking directly into the camera with a shy, affectionate smile, the same to-die-for smile she'd given me when I asked her to marry me.

Now, as I stared into Claire's eyes, her final words came involuntarily to mind: "I'm seeing someone." What little appetite I'd had was gone. Probably, she'd been "seeing someone" when this picture was made. Had she given him that same smile? Had she, earlier that day of her fortieth birthday, shared a private moment with him so he could wish her a happy birthday?

I looked over at Allie. She was looking down at a nearly full plate of food, not making a move to eat any more of it. I hadn't known what to expect, but I certainly didn't expect this silence between us. Was she still angry with me for "forgetting" the birthday? Or was there more? I'd tried to talk to her when we first sat down to the simple meal that had been one of Claire's favorites: garlicky grilled chicken, mashed potatoes and spinach sautéed with butter. Allie had been unresponsive, staring straight ahead, never quite looking at the picture of Claire that drew my eyes like a radioactive magnet.

"Daddy?" Allie said, her face gone pale.

"Yes?" My voice was too loud.

"Can I leave the table now?" Even though her food had been more re-arranged than eaten.

I wrangled my voice into a softer tone. "You haven't eaten much, Sweetpea."

"Don't call me that."

It felt like a slap in the face. "Allie, are you okay?"

Tears now. "What do you *think*, Paul?" She bolted from the table, nearly knocking her chair to the floor. She ran through the family room, stopped to pick up Onesie from the sofa, then continued into her bedroom. The bedroom door closed with a bang.

"Paul." She'd never called me that before. I could hardly believe it now. I felt with Allie just as I'd occasionally felt with Claire, that I'd hurt her and didn't know how, and because of this I must be shunned. I looked again at Claire's picture. I wished she were here now. She would be able to tell me what Allie had been feeling when she fled the table, would know what to do about it. I didn't know whether to pursue Allie or give her time and space. Given the way she'd called me "Paul," I decided I'd better wait a bit before knocking on her door.

Unable to finish my meal, I recalled how Claire and I had first met. She'd been the wife of a couple who'd come for help with their marriage. I'd been drawn to Claire immediately—she was thin, with full breasts and a killer sense of humor. Subtle, but oh, so sharp. I'd been able to tell before the hour was up that the marriage she'd brought me to repair was beyond help. Way beyond. Andrew, Claire's husband, had come to the session only to appease her, or perhaps to demonstrate to a judge he'd done his best to try to make the marriage work. They'd come for just that one session, which was how I later justified to myself it was okay to date her. She hadn't *really* been a patient. I'd never seen her in individual psychotherapy, nor for an extended period of time. Just that once, and her husband had done most of the talking.

We'd met for the second time a year later through an online dating service. She'd been suggested to me as an "ideal match" by the dating site's algorithm. I reached out to her on a whim, wondering if the same algorithm had presented me to her. I sent her a short electronic note in which I remarked on the coincidence of a patient and therapist being matched as an "ideal couple." I hadn't expected a response but was pleased when she wrote back to say—well, how much of a patient had she been, after all? Wouldn't it be okay to meet for coffee?

We'd gone to the local Starbucks. I was thirty-two; she, twenty-nine, though she looked younger. She was shy, and insecure in an endearing way. "I can't believe I invited my *therapist* to have coffee with me," she said. "How weird is that?" Over coffee we discovered mutual interests in hiking, reading, bird-watching. The coffee led to a movie date that weekend, then to dinner and drinks at my apartment the next, and the third weekend to my bed. I was transported during our first sexual experience but couldn't tell how she'd experienced it. This should have been a clue. I would later discover that in nearly everything, Claire held a reserve. She was always glad to see me, glad to spend time together, occasionally over-the-moon happy, but most of the time it was hard to tell how she really felt. Except when she was angry, which in the early days was rare. I'd often felt *this close* to seeing her, to really knowing her, but I could count on one hand the times when the fog lifted and she was really, fully, there. I loved her more dearly every time this happened. I continued to hope, even expect, a time would come when she would be more available.

Now, as I sat at the table with only her picture for company, I wondered if the man she might have started dating toward the end of her life had been able to find her at last, to *know* her in a way I never had. *Probably not,* I thought. *Claire could not help being Claire.*

Allie had been alone long enough. So had I. I paused outside her door and gave a light knock. No response. "Allie?" I said. Nothing. I said her name a little louder, made a couple more raps on the door. Still nothing. I tried to turn the handle of the doorknob, but it wouldn't turn. She locked me out? *Really?* I made my hand into a fist and knocked more firmly. "Allie please, let me in." There was a tick of sound in the doorknob and I was able to turn it. By the time I was inside the room, she'd already returned to her bed. She was facing away from me, toward a wall that featured a rainbow painted in bright colors. A single bluebird flew through the rainbow's high arch.

I remembered Claire helping Allie choose the colors for the wall and apply their correct rainbow sequence: red on top, then yellow, orange, green, dark purple, with violet at the bottom. I recalled Allie's delight when the mural was complete. Claire had added the bird in flight as an afterthought. "Is the bird, *me,* Mommy?" Allie had asked. Claire said yes, of course it was.

I sat next to Allie. I wanted to put my hand on her back but was pretty sure she didn't want to be touched now. Especially by me, though I still couldn't fathom what I'd done to put her off. I placed my hand on Onesie, who had curled against Allie. At my touch, the little cat stood, walked out of reach and began to bathe herself, as though she too didn't want any part of me. I called Allie's name.

She took a sharp intake of breath and let out a single, coughing sob. When she spoke, her voice was soft but firm. "Who was driving the car?"

I was stunned even as I knew exactly what she was asking. I didn't want to answer. I suspected she knew the answer already, might have known it for a long time, but I didn't want to say it. "I was," I said, tears stinging my eyes. I didn't let them fall. This wasn't about *my* feelings.

Allie took another breath and with it came a cry so fraught with pain I flinched and Onesie jumped to the floor. Allie pulled herself into a tight ball, her knees close against her chest. I understood both her anguish and her anger. At fate. At me. But there was something else, too. She needed me.

After a minute or two, with Allie still faced away from me, she spoke again, her voice much younger than her age. "How did it happen?"

I was prepared. "I ran a red light."

She startled and turned to look at me, her eyes dark with judgement.

"I was distracted by something your mother told me." I said this without thinking, and as soon as I said it, I knew I'd painted myself into an impossible corner.

"What did she say?"

The lie I would have to tell Allie now would forever separate her from the truth, and in a way, from me. Yet I had to tell it. If I were to let Allie know what her mother had actually said, that she was seeing someone else and wanted a divorce, Claire would become in Allie's nine-year-old mind the one to blame. I wouldn't do that to her or to Claire. "She said she was unhappy."

Allie angled her head to the side, puzzled. "More than usual?"

Allie had known about Claire's tendency toward depression? "Well, yes," I said. "More than usual and I wanted to know why. So I turned to look at her, and when I did, I missed the light turning red."

Allie thought for a minute and then said, "It takes a long time for a light to go from green, to yellow, to red."

A simple truth. "Yes, it does. It's just that the expression on your mother's face...I don't know, it captured me somehow."

Surprisingly, Allie appeared to understand this, as though she, too, had known such moments with her mother, moments when she'd studied Claire to puzzle out what was going on behind the veil. For a long time Allie didn't speak, her eyes focused on some distant place. When she did speak again, her voice was flat. "You were driving and you took your eyes off the road."

The terrible weight of this simple fact, seen for the first time through Allie's eyes, hit me in a way it never had before. A dark well of dread opened within me, the dread of being forever banished from

Allie's heart, and it brought with it a depression I thought might stay with me the rest of my days. Allie squeezed her eyes hard together and turned back toward the wall with the rainbow and bluebird. I had to believe she wanted me to stay and not leave, so I sat beside her as her body swelled and contracted in silent, furtive sobs. I remained with her until her breathing slowed, and after a long while took on the measured rhythm of sleep.

I felt as helpless then and as sick with guilt as when I'd been at the morgue, seeing Claire's lifeless body. I'd discovered something that day, that there is an incomprehensibility at the heart of life: an essential, inscrutable enigma that will not answer why a certain thing has happened, only declare that it has. I'd done my best to move on from that day. I knew I would have to move on from this day as well. I rose from Allie's bed and went to my chair in the living room, where I sat for a long time, numbly worrying about what tomorrow would bring.

The next morning when I arrived at Allie's room, her door was closed. I was sure I'd left it open. She must have awakened during the night and shut it. I opened the door quietly, intending to wake her as I always had.

Allie was sitting at her desk, dressed for school and hunched over her laptop. It was a shock, the way she'd separated herself from our usual morning rituals. In that moment I felt something immeasurably precious had been taken from me, that I'd lost some part of Allie. Some part of myself. "You should knock when the door's closed," Allie said, not looking up, her fingers playing across her laptop's keyboard.

"I'm sorry," I said, still hardly believing she was already up and dressed. "What kind of french toast do you want this morning?"

She looked at me with an expression I couldn't decipher. It wasn't exactly hurt, or defiance, or regret, but contained a bit of all three. "I'll fix myself some cereal."

I left and closed the door. I remembered Allie's preoccupation with the frailty of planet earth and all the living things it held within its carefully modulated warmth. "One day," she'd said, during one of our conversations about it, "it will all be over." I hadn't really understood her despair. Now, I felt it too.

After dropping a silent Allie off at school and driving to my office, I had an hour to kill before my first appointment. I had things to do, but all I could manage was to sit in my chair, weighed down by what had happened between Allie and me. "You were driving and you took your eyes off the road." She'd said it like an indictment, and I was already getting a glimpse of what my sentence would be: solitary confinement within my own home.

I had taken my eyes off the road. I remembered that. But what happened after had always been a blur of fragmented recollections. As though I were in a trance, a succession of memories began to play in my mind like a horror I'd tried but failed to escape.

CHAPTER EIGHT

"I need to tell you something."

Claire, speaking from the passenger seat of my Toyota Camry as we were stuck in traffic on our way back from a routine trip to the grocery store. The tone of her voice was low, hesitant, suggesting this might be the beginning of an uncomfortable conversation. I glanced at her briefly, long enough to see her take a breath and look down, her dark blonde hair falling across her cheek. I thought she was going to tell me she'd decided to go with her sister to New Orleans for a long weekend together—something she and I had argued about the day before. I'd asked why she wanted to make the trip. After all, she and her sister hadn't been close in many years. She'd said that's exactly why she wanted to go—to *get* close.

In the car, I saw Claire look up, but not at me. "I can't do this anymore," she said, as though letting go a thought she'd been holding in a long time. Everyone knows what it means when a spouse says, "I can't do this anymore." But she couldn't mean *that.* We'd been through a rough patch, I knew; for the better part of a year, we'd spent little time together apart from time with Allie. But Claire was as much a part of me as my own name; I couldn't imagine life without her. I was about to ask what she meant when she spoke the last words I would ever hear her say.

"I'm seeing someone."

I looked over at her, intending to ask her to repeat what she'd said, even though the sick, alarmed feeling in my gut knew exactly what she meant. She turned toward me with a bloom of compassion in her blue-green eyes and I could tell she was about to say something that would hurt. I braced myself for it—and through the window behind her caught a glimpse of an impossibly large truck approaching much too fast.

I came to in a daze. My body ached, my chest hurt from where the seat belt and airbag had saved my life. At first I didn't comprehend what had happened. I looked around, trying to get my bearings. Our car was surrounded by other cars and by people gathering in the street. Then I remembered the whelming blur of movement to my right, a sense of *too late* gripping my gut, the deafening sound of a mighty horn. Tires screaming across pavement. A violent collision spinning us helplessly around as my air bag slammed me hard against the seat.

Claire, where was she? I pushed aside the spent airbag and looked next to me. The only thing I could see was the mangled front of a semi-truck wed steel on steel with the right front of my car, the passenger door partially open. The passenger seat empty. I wanted only one thing: to rewind time.

A paramedic appeared, young, strapping, blue-eyed. He helped me out the driver's side door, where the smell of something burning made it hard to breathe. Strangers stood in a loose circle, their faces showing shock and concern. A tall man, thin and rough-looking, angry, pointed at me, shouting "...ran the fucking red light." The man said something else, but his words were drowned out by the sound of sirens fast approaching.

In a panic I scanned the area for Claire but couldn't find her. She had to be *somewhere.* A police car stopped a few yards away. Two cops exited the car. One of them, his blue uniform bright in the afternoon sun, asked the paramedic if I was okay. "We'd like to ask him some questions."

"Give us a minute," the paramedic said.

I turned to him. "My wife. Where is she?" The man didn't answer but pointed to a stretcher being loaded into an ambulance many yards away. Filled with hope and fear, I got there just as the door closed. "Where are you taking her?" I asked the man who had closed the door.

"Jackson Hospital."

"Can I—"

"I'm sorry sir. We don't allow ride-alongs." He gestured behind me. The policemen had followed me to the back of the ambulance.

Questions. They had questions. I had questions, too. Had I really taken my eyes off the road long enough to miss the light turning yellow and then red? I had no recollection of the light changing color, only Claire's last words and after that, as I struggled to take in their meaning, an expression on her face that suggested she was about to say more. I felt desperate now to know what it was she'd wanted to say.

"Excuse me, sir. Can you tell us what happened here?" It was the taller of the two policemen, the one with a black moustache that matched his coal-black hair. He'd spoken with affected patience, as though to a child.

I told the cops I'd been talking with my wife one minute and the next thing I remembered was coming to after the accident. I acted like I didn't know what had happened. But I knew: I took my eyes off the road. And in that span of time where I was grappling to come to terms with what Claire had told me, looking to her face for clues, a stoplight led by a blind timing device blinked twice. An ugly thought crossed my mind. *Did I do it on purpose?* Had Claire's words, *I'm seeing someone,* cut so deeply I wanted to blow our lives apart? Surely not. There hadn't been a split second for me to decide anything, much less something so horrific.

I was still in a daze as the cops handed me a citation for reckless driving then dropped me off at the Jackson Hospital emergency facility. A nurse summoned an older man with kind brown eyes. "My name is David. I'm a chaplain." I saw the serious look on David's face and my heart fell. Claire must have been very badly injured. I prepared myself mentally as David led me into a room where a doctor quickly appeared and told me the medical team had done everything possible to save my wife but regrettably, they'd lost her. None of this could be true.

David asked if I wanted to see Claire. Absolutely not. I didn't want my final image of her to be whatever she looked like now. But, of course, I had to see her. David led me to a room where a small, elderly woman with wiry grey hair stood by a gurney. Lying there was a body covered with a white hospital sheet. I was cold with fear as the woman lifted the sheet. Claire's head was covered with bloodied bandages, the right side of her face red and badly swollen. I stepped closer, wanting to help her somehow, but she was beyond me now. I could see that. The left side of her face was untouched. I rested my hand there, on her cheek, looking for a final connection. Her skin was unnaturally yielding; Claire was there but not there.

David practically had to carry me to his office, where he sat with me until my weeping subsided. He asked if I wanted to talk about Claire or call anyone. I thought of Claire's parents and her sister, but Claire hadn't been close to either and no way could I bear to tell them what had happened. What I'd done.

"No one you'd like to talk to?" the chaplain asked again.

My father. He would understand my predicament. But… I looked at David and told him my parents had died a few years back in the crash of a private plane.

"I'm so sorry."

"He was the pilot." I gave David a meaningful look, and he got it. I wondered what my parents had been talking about right before the plane went down. Had they, too, been arguing about something, their last minutes together lost in futile anger? Not likely. So far as I knew, they'd become a genuinely happy couple, especially after my Dad had a brief affair. I'd gathered from things he'd told me that the affair had served as a cautionary moment for them both. A yellow light, so to speak. Which they'd both had the sense to see and then stop their respective ways of hurting one another.

I thought of Roger, my closest friend and a colleague. What would I tell him? *I killed Claire?* What would Roger say to that? He'd want to know how and why it happened, and he'd have some understanding of my predicament. That would be a help. But Roger was out of the country. On honeymoon.

"There's no one to call."

David gave me the name and number of a funeral director, and I made an appointment to meet the following day at the funeral home. Then David summoned a cab to take me home.

Home. How could it ever seem that way again? Allie would return from school in less than an hour. In the cab, I pulled out my phone and googled, "How to tell a child her mother has died." There were no magic answers, only bits of advice I already knew. Be simple, be direct. Help the child name her feelings. Share your own. I couldn't imagine how I might begin the conversation, or when. Right away? Or after giving her a drink and a snack. For a semi-psychotic moment, I thought Claire would be able to help me make these decisions. She was so much better at this sort of thing than I.

Then I realized I was on my own in this—on my own in everything now—and I wished I had died in the accident instead of Claire.

CHAPTER NINE

Three days after Allie confronted me about the accident in which her mother died, we sat together at the breakfast table, me reading the morning paper while she looked at her phone. We'd finished eating many minutes before, Allie having made herself cereal as she had the past three mornings. Yesterday and the day before, Allie's attitude toward me had been cordial, but cool. I didn't know what to do but wait for something to change.

I put the paper down and watched her text back and forth, probably to Liz, one of the few girls her age who also had a cellphone. It occurred to me she could just as easily do this in her room. Did her staying at the table point to some bit of connective tissue still left between us? Or was she simply too preoccupied to move? "Where's my book bag?" she asked casually, not looking up as she worked her fingers on the phone's keypad.

"Did you take it out of the car when you got home from school yesterday?" I asked.

"Oh, maybe not." She put the phone down and left the table.

I rose from my chair and started clearing the dishes. From across the house, I heard Allie shout, "Onesie! *No.*" Then to me,

"Come. *Quick*." I set the dishes down and rushed to the back of the house. The door to the garage was open, along with the garage door itself. Allie was nowhere in sight. I'd opened the garage door earlier to retrieve some cat food from the trunk of my car, which was parked in the driveway outside. I thought I knew what had happened: When Allie opened the door into the garage to get her book bag from the car, Onesie had escaped.

I could hear Allie calling for the kitten from around the side of the house. When I reached her, she confirmed Onesie had gotten out and my heart sank. It was my fault for leaving the garage door open, another thoughtless mistake, and what would this do to Allie's already grim opinion of me? I was about to apologize when she said, "I wasn't careful. I didn't check to see where Onesie was before I opened the door." Her voice broke. "She's gone, Daddy."

The "Daddy" surprised me. "Cats don't usually stray too far from home," I told her. "I think she'll be back."

Onesie had never been outside the house. I'd thought she would be an indoor/outdoor cat, but Allie wouldn't have it; she didn't want to risk Onesie getting hit by a car. She hadn't said the words, but I knew what she'd been thinking. *Like Mom was.* I helped her look for the cat. It felt good to be doing something together, but when the time came for me to take Allie to school, we still hadn't found Onesie.

"What if Onesie comes back while I'm at school and you're at work and no one is here to let her in?" Allie asked.

I placed my hand on her shoulder, the first time I'd touched her in three days. "I think she'll hang around until we get back."

• • •

A little after noon, Angela sat across from Dr. Paul willing herself not to shake. A minute or two ago, Dr. Paul had asked her what was on her mind. She didn't know where or how to start. First, there was her disturbing discovery that Ricardo had come to this office, perhaps sat in this very chair. Then there was Michael. He hadn't shown for their date. She'd tried several times to contact him and—nothing. She was beyond worried.

"What are you thinking?" Dr. Paul asked.

She felt if she spoke, her words would make Michael's disappearance real, not just a fear in her mind. She looked up from her shoes to Dr. Paul's face, and when she did, she could see he looked tired. Of course. He had a life, too. Maybe things weren't going so well. "You look tired," she said.

"I am, a little."

She looked down again, at her red sneakers. "I guess you have problems, too."

"Do you wonder if I'm too tired to work with you today?"

"Not really. Just stalling."

There was affection in his eyes now, and a trace of amusement.

"This isn't funny," she said, the words coming out harsher than she'd intended. The amusement left his eyes, and for an instant he looked hurt.

"I didn't think it was funny," he said, his eyes lit with concern. "I think you must be troubled about something."

A ball of lead rolled from her chest into her gut and settled there. She looked away from Dr. Paul's unwavering eyes. "Michael is missing."

The doctor sat up a little straighter. "What do you mean, missing?"

It took effort to form the words. "We were supposed to meet night before last. He never showed and when I called his cell he didn't answer. He didn't answer my texts either, so yesterday I drove by his apartment. His car was there, but he didn't come out when I rang the bell. Then I went by the gym where he works. He hadn't show up for work yesterday, or the day before." Suddenly, the room felt cold and she began to tremble. She didn't tell Dr. Paul about her frantic call to Ricardo, who of course denied any knowledge of Michael's whereabouts.

Dr. Paul leaned forward in his chair. "Angela, what do you *think* happened to Michael?"

"I don't know." It was the truth, but not the whole truth.

"Do you have an idea about what *might* have happened?"

She nodded, waiting for him to pull it out of her, but he said nothing more. No need to hide Ricardo's real name any longer. "The last time I saw Ricardo, he told me he knew who it was I've been seeing. I'm afraid he's done something."

"Something?"

She closed her eyes, remembering Ricardo's words when she first told him she wanted to leave: *Quitting me is not an option.* She opened her eyes again and asked the doctor if he had read in the paper last year about an undercover cop getting killed in a crack house.

"Yes, I read about that."

"That was Ricardo's doing. Not personally, but he ordered the hit." A look of alarm passed through Dr. Paul's eyes and she realized she'd just told him about a murder. An *unsolved* murder. And she'd told him who'd done it. "Look, forget I said that. I shouldn't have."

"It doesn't work that way, Angela. I can't pretend not to know this."

"Are you going to have to report what I said? Aren't there, like, privacy laws?"

"There are such laws, but there are exceptions. If you told me *you'd* killed someone, I'd have to report it, or convince you to. But I'm pretty sure what you told me is considered 'hearsay.' So no, I don't have to report it." His voice took on an urgency. "But you're telling me Ricardo is capable of murder. So, what about Michael? Have you called the police?"

"Why?" she said. "To tell them a friend is missing? I have no evidence anything's gone wrong."

"Still, you could make a report, let them know your concern."

She looked away, slowly shaking her head. "You don't understand."

He leaned toward her. "What don't I understand?"

How could she explain Ricardo, who lived in a world without normal rules, to a man like Dr. Paul? "You don't know what he's capable of," she said, letting out a breath she didn't realize she'd been holding. "One time, he wanted me to go with him to a club. I didn't want to go. His driver was there and when Ricardo started to drag me out the door, the driver stopped him. Ricardo grabbed a letter opener from a table by the door and stabbed his driver in the chest. I ran to the bathroom, locked the door and called 911. The paramedics came and the police, but Ricardo was more annoyed than concerned, even when the police took him away. He came back after a few hours and told me that at the police station he'd made one call—*one phone call*—and it was as if the whole thing had never happened."

Dr. Paul looked worried. "So—he's beyond the law?"

"He's beyond Miami law, that's for sure."

Dr. Paul had a funny look on his face, as if he'd swallowed something distasteful. "Angela," he said, "Ricardo came by my office last week."

Hearing him say this, even though she knew it to be true, made Ricardo's violation more real. "I know. He told me."

"Did he tell you he threatened me?"

A feeling of nausea took hold in her stomach as she tried to sort out what the doctor had said. "He threatened you?"

Dr. Paul's eyes became hard. "I have a nine-year-old daughter. Ricardo told me where she goes to school, who her teachers are."

Angela stopped breathing. Maybe *she* didn't know what Ricardo was capable of.

Dr. Paul rolled his chair closer. "We have to figure out what to do." He didn't seem like a therapist anymore. He was just a man, a father, the father of a little girl who might be in danger. No way could he continue to be her therapist. Abruptly, she stood and left the office, not stopping when Dr. Paul called her name.

• • •

The scent of Angela's perfume lingered, as did the chilling effect of what I'd learned about Ricardo, the violence he was capable of and the powerful connections he must have. I'd acted unprofessionally when I told Angela about Ricardo's session and the threat he'd made. Patient confidentiality and all that. But I wanted to get Angela's read on the man; I hadn't known how seriously to take his threats. What Angela told me shook me to the core. I wanted to believe there was another explanation for why Michael had disappeared, but when I recalled Ricardo's face, the depth of hatred in his eyes, I believed he was indeed responsible for Michael's disappearance. The evil in

Ricardo seemed infinite, the way love can be, and the more I thought about the situation I was in, the more frightened I became. There was no way I could continue to work with Angela, and anyone I might refer her to would be in the same position as I was. Ricardo would threaten them too, and their families.

Driving home at the end of the day, I remembered about Onesie, how she'd gone missing. I expected to find her sleeping by the front door or behind the house, and as I pulled into the driveway I scanned the yard. No little cat. I got out of the car and walked around the house, calling Onesie's name. She wasn't by the back door, either. Then, as I came around to the front yard again, I saw her lying in a neighbor's yard just off the street. I rushed over and put my hand on her, hoping to feel a heartbeat or a breath, but there was no murmur of greeting, no responsive meow, only a surprising stiffness. She must have been hit by a car. I took my hand away and closed my eyes, thinking of all the hope Onesie had brought to Allie's life and mine.

I lifted Onesie from the grass and carried her rigid body through the garage into the kitchen. Not knowing what else to do, I laid her in the sink. I thought about burying her in the backyard before Allie got home, letting her believe Onesie might still be alive and might one day return to us.

"Hi, Daddy."

I jumped at the sound of Allie's voice. She'd come in through the open garage.

"*Scared* you, didn't I?" She was laughing.

The simple delight in her voice, the bit of affection it held after so much distance, and the knowledge of what I had to tell her brought tears to my eyes.

"What's the matter?" she asked. I was still looking at Onesie in the sink, my back to Allie.

"I found Onesie," I said, turning toward her.

Allie's face lit up, her eyes expanding like little blue balloons—until she saw what was in my eyes. Her body went rigid. I took Onesie out of the sink and laid her on the kitchen floor. "Nooooo," Allie cried. She bent down to stroke the kitten, her tears falling onto Onesie's lifeless body. I sat cross-legged beside her on the kitchen floor until she could speak again. "Daddy," she asked, her voice barely there, her face ruined with grief.

"Yes?"

"What happened?"

"I think she was hit by a car."

Allie was silent for moments as she took this in. Then she asked if we could bury Onesie in the backyard.

I was grateful I hadn't buried the cat without her or lied about Onesie's death. We went outside and dug a hole, Allie using a trowel for her share of the work. Together we lifted the kitten from the kitchen floor, carried her outside and lowered her into the ground. Then we covered her with broken dirt and grass and—this was Allie's idea—set a cross of twigs above where she lay.

In the dinner that followed neither of us spoke much, but the earlier tension between us seemed to have drained away. We treated each other gently, as though both of us had survived a terrible accident. Which of course we had.

When Allie went to bed she kept her bedroom door open for the first time in three nights, and while I was reading in the living room she called out to ask if I would bring her a glass of water. She'd never done that before. I drew the water, giving silent thanks to

Onesie for having brought about, even in her death, a renewed connection between Allie and me.

The next morning, just as I was coming awake, I felt an undefined fear clawing at my gut. I sat up to get my bearings and realized where the fear was coming from: the realization that Allie was in danger. I'd already made the decision not to work with Angela any longer but hadn't told her yet. I decided I didn't want to wait three days until her next appointment to do so. Better to defuse any threat from Ricardo sooner than later. I would call Angela today and ask her to come in as soon as possible. Even though it went against every professional fiber of my being to cut her loose, I had to. To make sure my head was on straight, I'd call Roger, a friend and colleague, to get a consultation. But I didn't think anyone could talk me out of letting Angela go.

With that settled, I felt better. Keeping in mind Onesie's death yesterday and its effect upon Allie, I decided to look in on her to see if she was awake yet. When I stepped inside her dim room, it looked for one heart-stopping moment as though her bed were empty, but then I saw her tightly balled up in the covers. I put my hand on her.

She wasn't there after all.

CHAPTER TEN

With accelerating panic I searched every room, even the closets, calling Allie's name. She was nowhere to be found. Then I thought I knew where she must be: outside, at Onesie's grave. This made so much sense I felt relieved—until she wasn't there, either.

I allowed myself to think the impossible. Might Ricardo have sent men to take her in the night, a job so professional I hadn't been awakened? I was about to call the police when I realized I'd better not. If I told the police Allie was missing and might have been abducted, they'd want to know if I had any suspects. If Ricardo truly was "beyond Miami law," contacting the police might make things worse for Allie. I had to take another path. I tapped the icon for "contacts" on my phone and then the link to Angela's number.

"Angela," I said, my breath quickening, "my daughter is missing. Do you think it's possible Ricardo might have taken her?" It felt wrong to be intruding into Angela's life like this, calling her early in the morning asking for help even though I was no longer willing to help her. But I needed to know.

"Let me look into it," she said. "I'll call you back when I know more."

• • •

Angela didn't think Ricardo had taken Dr. Paul's daughter. Before he did something like that, he would wait until he'd had a chance to find out whether or not his threat had been effective. Let the threat play out, see what happens. That was how he worked.

Ricardo had spent the night before downtown after a series of late meetings. Angela rang his cell. When Ricardo answered, she told him she'd just spoken to Paul Mason. "Meet me at the condo," she said. She intended to ask him about Dr. Paul's daughter, but what she really wanted to know was what he had done to Michael.

Thirty minutes later, after she'd gotten dressed and had a bite to eat, Ricardo came through the door. Angela was waiting for him on the sofa. He walked toward her, but before he had a chance to sit next to her, she held out her hand like a stop sign and asked, "Do you have the girl?" It was a calculatedly vague question. If he'd taken Dr. Paul's daughter, he would know what she was talking about. If not, he wouldn't have a clue.

"Excuse me?" he said, his face the picture of puzzlement.

"Dr. Mason's daughter. Where is she?"

He was standing in front of her now, shrugging his shoulders. "How do I know this?"

"Dr. Mason says you threatened him. He said you know where his daughter goes to school, who her teachers are."

Understanding came into Ricardo's face and he visibly relaxed. "I meant to scare the doctor, that is all. And demonstrate how much

I love you, how far I will go to keep you in my life." He smiled now, the earnest lover.

The smile turned her stomach. "It doesn't *feel* like love, Ricardo."

He sat down next to her and touched her affectionately on the cheek. "It is true I like to control what I love."

She brushed his hand away. "And what about Michael? Where is he?" She could feel her stomach tighten.

Ricardo smiled smugly. "Ah, yes, the man you had such high hopes for."

His attitude was—what was the word? Galling. That was it. She pictured Michael the last time they'd been together. After they'd said goodbye and he'd walked away, he turned and gave her a look of love she would never forget. "*Where,* Ricardo?" she asked again.

He raised an eyebrow. "You thought he cared about you, no?"

She looked down, unable to speak the words foremost in her mind: *How badly did you hurt him?*

"Let me put you at ease," Ricardo said. "You overestimated this man. You thought you mattered to him. I spoke with him and after our conversation he agreed to relocate to another city. Another state, actually." Ricardo leaned toward her and snapped his fingers. "Just like *that,* he cut you off like the dead branch of a worthless tree."

She turned to face Ricardo, willing herself not to cry. "Did you hurt him?"

"It did not take much to persuade him to go."

Angela knew Ricardo would never tell her what it had "taken" to get Michael to leave. Ricardo was not a man who showed his cards. But no doubt, he'd hurt Michael. She remembered she'd seen Michael's car in the parking lot of his apartment building. Surely Michael wouldn't "vamoose" without his car. She was about to tell

Ricardo she'd seen the car when he moved suddenly closer and ran his fingers through her hair, the lovely scent of his expensive cologne coming off him like a lie because there was nothing lovely about him at all. When he moved to kiss her on the lips, she had a mind to slap him but thought of something better. She brought her lips to his and when he pushed his disgusting tongue into her mouth, she bit down on it. Hard.

He bellowed and pulled away, pushing her against the sofa with such force she thought she might have blacked out for a moment. As he staggered to his feet, she discovered there was part of him still in her mouth. She spit it into her hand, a fleshy, bloody mass a quarter inch long and shocking to see. Ricardo slurred curses at her—*bitch* you *fucking bitch*—as he ran to the kitchen, blood leaking from his lips. She knew she'd better be gone when he returned.

She was halfway to the door when he rounded the corner, his mouth smeared with blood, a bag of ice in his hand. He caught her from behind and pushed her to the floor. She scrambled on hands and knees in a desperate attempt to reach the door, but he grabbed her by the leg, turned her over and pulled her to him, pinning her arms beneath his knees. She was prey now, looking up at her captor, his blood dripping onto her face as he slapped her hard across the cheek, slapping every thought out of her frightened mind and then slapping her again, a dark hunger in his black eyes. There was blood in *her* mouth now, and blood on her face where her nose was surely broken. Just when she thought she might black out, just as she was hoping for that dark oblivion, he rose and stood above her.

"You are dead to me," he told her, a murderous tone in his voice.

• • •

I searched for another explanation for Allie's disappearance. What if it had nothing to do with Ricardo? She'd gone to bed brokenhearted. Might she have awakened early, still in grief, and gone to Biscayne Bay to feel close to her mother? God knows she needed Claire after a day like yesterday. Claire's favorite spot on the bay was only four blocks away. I took off running, my mind telling me: *Be prepared; she might not be there.* After one or two minutes I saw her a block ahead, walking toward me with her head down, the iconic motherless child. She noticed me and stopped walking as I ran on toward her. It occurred to me she'd left home without leaving a note. Had she done so on purpose? When I reached her, I asked, "Did you go to the bay to feel close to Mommy?" Looking down, she nodded her head. "Did you tell her about Onesie?" Another nod. "I'm so sorry, Allie."

She said something I couldn't quite make out. I asked her to repeat it. The words came slowly, each one barely audible. "It was… my… *fault*."

"What do you mean it was your fault? *I* left the garage door open."

"No," she said, her voice louder now. I knew the garage door was open. I'd gone out there earlier to get some clothes from the dryer."

It was all too clear what Allie must be feeling: that she was responsible for Onesie's death. Just as I was responsible for Claire's. I moved to pull her into an embrace, but she shook her head. As I watched her small figure walk away, head down, I noticed for the first time what a beautiful morning it was. It struck me how indifferent the world can be, to go about strutting its glory in the face of immeasurable heartbreak and loss. I caught up with Allie and walked beside her, telling myself, as I'd told myself countless times before, that somehow we would make it through this newly rent tear in the still frail fabric of our lives.

CHAPTER ELEVEN

I walked beside Allie, neither of us speaking, her taking two and three strides to my one. In the distance a baby cried and I remembered Allie as a toddler attempting her first, stiff-legged steps. I was the one she'd been trying to reach. On the third try she'd made it, squealing with wide-eyed delight as she threw her arms around my neck. I longed for that little girl now, the Allie that loved me unconditionally.

It was getting warm out and the combination of my run to find Allie and my jangled nerves had created a sweat. I would need to shower before taking her to school and myself to work. Maybe, I thought, we could both play hooky, spend the day together. Half a block from home, my cellphone pinged with a text message from Angela. "Spoke 2 Ricardo. He doesn't have Ur daughter." I tapped a quick response: "Allie with me now. Thx so much :)" I regretted calling Angela and with Allie safely beside me, no longer felt it urgent to inform Angela right away of my decision to terminate our work together. I would wait and tell her at our regular session on Monday.

Allie and I were at the front door when I thought again about the fact she hadn't left a note to let me know where she'd gone. I didn't believe she'd simply forgotten to do so. For some reason, she'd intended me to worry. I made french toast while she retreated to her bedroom and then after breakfast I made calls to reschedule my appointments for the day. It was Friday, typically a paperwork day, so there were only three appointments to change.

"Why are you changing your appointments?" Allie asked.

"I thought we could spend the day together."

She put her fork down and frowned. "What about school?" Her eyes little blue judges, calling me out of order.

"School will be there on Monday," I said. She looked at me, serious but not sad, as though waiting to see what other surprises I might have in store. "If you really want to go to school today, though, I'll take you."

She looked away, in the direction of the school. "No, I'll stay here. But what will we do?" Her forehead wrinkled.

I didn't have a plan, but I had ideas. I told Allie we could go to the zoo, or have ice cream on the beach, or go shopping. I could tell by her flat expression that none of these possibilities hit home. I asked if there was anything she'd like to do.

She looked at me uncertainly. "I only don't want to go to school because I'm afraid of seeing Liz."

"You mean because of what happened to Onesie?"

Allie shrugged and looked down at her plate of unfinished french toast.

"How about this," I said. "When school is out, I'll take you to Liz's house and explain I left the garage door open and Onesie got out and had a terrible accident. How about we do that?"

Allie's face melted in relief. "So…I can go to school then?"

"If we hurry," I said, trying to sound upbeat, "we can beat the bell." I was disappointed she didn't want to spend the day with me but didn't say anything. I took her to school and then continued on to my office. There was insurance to file, notes to complete, bills to pay. I found the work calming and was just as glad I didn't have patients to see. When doing therapy, I relied on my emotions to provide a kind of radar to divine the subtle, unspoken depths of a patient's psyche. Today, my emotions were too roiled to do that well. Probably, that's one of the reasons I'd been so quick to reschedule. I needed time to settle from the loss of Onesie, from Allie's grief about it, and from the impossible situation I was in with Angela and Ricardo.

At the end of the day, as I was putting things in order before going grocery shopping and picking Allie up from school, the bell rang indicating an arrival in the waiting room. I was sure I'd left a message for my final appointment of the day, asking her to call to reschedule. I opened the door expecting to see an overweight, thirty-seven-year-old woman. Instead, there sat Ricardo Raphael, impeccably dressed in a three-piece suit. I froze in the doorway.

"Dr. Mason, could I trouble you for one moment?"

He sounded different than before, almost as though he had something in his mouth he was talking around. "What do you want, Ricardo?" My words had come out louder than I'd intended.

"As I say, to speak with you." Ricardo stepped past me, gesturing for me to follow him into my office. Ricardo's movements were so smooth I nearly complied. Then I caught myself and told Ricardo we could talk in the waiting room. Ignoring me, he continued into the office and sat in one of the leather chairs. Angry at his intrusion, I took my customary seat and waited to hear what the man had to say.

Ricardo sat ramrod straight, but his eyes betrayed a discomfort I hadn't seen before. "I would like to work with you."

I was sure I'd misunderstood. When I didn't respond, he added, "As a patient."

The idea was so absurd I nearly laughed. "Not going to happen," I said, shaking my head.

Ricardo leaned forward and absent-mindedly rubbed the jagged scar above his right eye. "Dr. Mason, I will pay twice your normal fee."

"My fee is my fee. It's not negotiable."

"I meant no offense. I ask you to reconsider."

In spite of my apprehension at even being in the same room as Ricardo, I was intrigued. What could he possibly want to work on? And why with me? But I wasn't *that* intrigued. "No, Ricardo," I said. "I won't work with you."

Ricardo spread his hands wide apart. "Why not?"

"For one thing, you threatened me." It felt good to say this, to get it out on the table.

"Or you took some information I conveyed to be a threat." Ricardo's attitude had become condescending, as though he were correcting a subordinate. "In fact I did nothing to harm you, Dr. Mason. Nothing at all."

"You worried me. That's harm enough."

"Ah, yes. Angela told me you thought I had kidnapped your daughter. Have you found her, Dr. Mason? If not, I have resources. I could help you find her."

I let my anger show in my voice. "I found my daughter. And you told me last time we spoke that you know where she goes to school, what her schedule is. What was that if not a threat?"

Ricardo raised his hands in mock surrender. "You are correct. I did say things meant to persuade you to stop working with Angela." He looked at me dead on. "But I never would have done anything to hurt your daughter. I promise you that."

I indulged my curiosity. "Ricardo, what could you possibly want my help with?"

Ricardo sat forward in his chair, suddenly eager and speaking quickly. "As you may know, this morning Angela bit off part of my tongue." He made a show of sticking out his tongue, which ended in an ugly, ragged nub. I wondered how this had happened. "Normally," Ricardo said, "I would punish such an act. I believe in, not an eye for an eye, but *two* eyes for one." His face turned grave. "She needs to be burned. Whether with fire or acid, I have not decided. Fire has the advantage of drama. It stays in the mind. But acid disfigures so much more." He shook his head, looking genuinely perplexed. "The problem is, I cannot bring myself to do either one. I have thought about it all day—I have been able to think about nothing else—and I realize time alone will not change this. I could never hurt Angela that way. So, I need your help."

I was still focused on the brutality of what Ricardo had talked about. *Fire or acid?* Unbelievably, the man seemed serious about these things. And how, exactly, was he wanting me to help? "Wait a minute," I said. "You want me to work with you so you can be okay with the idea of hurting Angela?"

Ricardo smiled, his face softening. "It is not the way I would put it. It is more that I do not like being controlled. With Angela, something constrains me from handing her the punishment she deserves."

I held Ricardo's dark eyes for a moment before responding. "Why not just forget about her? Let her go?"

"I am constrained there as well. I cannot, as you say, 'forget about her.' Even now, although I have told her she is dead to me, I cannot stop thinking about her."

"When did this incident between the two of you happen?" I asked.

Ricardo settled back into the chair. "I told you. This morning. Very early."

It must have happened around the time I'd called Angela to ask for her help. Had my call somehow played a part in creating a situation where she'd bitten off the tip of Ricardo's tongue? And if it happened just this morning, how could Ricardo already be so sure he won't be able to take his revenge? "What you went through was traumatic," I told him. "Surely you haven't given yourself time to sort things out." When I realized the implications of what I'd said, I couldn't believe my stupidity. Had I just suggested that all the man needed was time to reach the point where he *could* take his revenge?

Ricardo's face tightened. "No offense, Dr. Mason, but you do not know me. I have been through far worse 'trauma' than what happened to me this morning. We will go over this when I am your patient. For me, the difficulty is not that she bit off part of my tongue. The difficulty is that I cannot do what I have always done in such a circumstance. To put it in words you might understand, I can no longer be myself."

I thought I did understand. No one but Angela had ever touched him so deeply. If this was true, Ricardo was at a turning point. He could either allow himself to be changed by this new experience or he could defend himself against it. Wall it off and return to his familiar way of being. He had in fact made a wise decision to seek therapy. But why me?

"Ricardo, why me? You could afford to work with anyone."

"I do not want to see just anyone. First, because I know you, the kind of man you are. Second, you know Angela, how special she is. Third, we have history already, you and me." He paused and looked slightly apologetic. "You know something about the kind of man I am."

I was more than fascinated: Here was a psychopathic mind challenged by the emergence of an apparently genuine, deeply seated care. Here was a chance to work on rarely seen ground. Of course, I couldn't work with Ricardo and certainly not while Angela was still a patient. I hadn't yet discharged her. More to myself than Ricardo, I said, "I can't do it."

Ricardo leaned forward. "Are you sure you want to make that decision before you hear what I have to offer?"

"I already told you. My fee is not negotiable."

Ricardo arched his eyebrows. "I do not speak of *your* fee, Dr. Mason. I am talking about, shall we say, *my* fee."

I had no idea what the man was talking about, but something about the way he'd said it sounded ominous. A chill ran through me.

"Should you refuse to work with me, that is," Ricardo continued.

My heartrate kicked up a notch. Did Ricardo mean what I thought he meant? Had he just turned the tables on me in a big—no—*spectacular* way?

Ricardo narrowed his eyes into slits of infinite darkness. "If you refuse to help me, your legs will be broken, both of them, in several places." He said this in a no-nonsense, matter-of-fact way. "After that, we will have nothing more to do with one another."

My mind was alive with images of an enormous hammer coming down on my leg. Both legs. I tried to settle myself, to slow my breathing, but I couldn't escape the panic coursing through my mind, my body. Nor could I look away from Ricardo's face, his dark, hideous eyes.

Then Ricardo's face suddenly changed and he broke into a grin. He put a hand on one knee and cocked his head to the side. "Did I have you going, Dr. Mason? If we are to work together, you must accustom yourself to my sense of humor."

I was angry now, more than angry. The speed with which Ricardo had changed course, the utter mastery of his emotions, was astonishing. One moment terrorizing, the next cajoling. I couldn't be sure which statement to believe: the threat, or his calling the threat a joke. "You were joking?" I said, loudly, showing Ricardo I didn't appreciate being jerked around.

"Of course. What kind of man do you think I am?" Ricardo then gave a sly, deliberate wink, which raised the question, did the wink mean the *joke* was a joke?

One thing I knew: I was unable to think clearly and was more afraid than I'd been in my life. The safest thing was to punt the ball, to play along and buy myself time to better assess the situation. I also realized I might be able to get something for Angela in the bargain.

"I set the ground rules," I said, sitting up straight and sounding surer of myself than I felt. "You tell me if you can live by them."

Ricardo had a pleased expression on his face. "Of course, Dr. Mason. Whatever you wish."

"We meet once a week, forty-five minutes each session. The fee is $165, payable at the beginning of the session, in cash. No calls to my home. And you must give Angela her freedom. She wants to be with you, fine. If she doesn't, you let her go." At the moment I felt more like an international diplomat than a therapist. Not a bad feeling, just different.

Ricardo waved his hand dismissively. "Yes, yes, I agree to these things. With one exception." I assumed the exception was going to be the idea of giving Angela her freedom. Ricardo looked at me in earnest. "I know you prefer to work in twice-weekly sessions. That is how often you were seeing Angela. That is what I want as well. I want your best, Dr. Mason, not some watered-down pretense."

With a nod I indicated I could live with that. Besides, I wasn't at all sure whether this was really going to happen. It certainly couldn't go on for long.

"When do we start?" Ricardo asked, beaming.

I said I had time at three o'clock on Monday. Ricardo stood and held out his hand. I stood and took it, then Ricardo turned and walked out the door.

Once Ricardo was gone, I had a feeling my mind—no, my *life*—had been hijacked. I returned to my chair. How could I work with someone I hated? And feared? I certainly couldn't buy into Ricardo's apparent goal: to recover enough of his "self" to punish Angela for what she'd done. I could hardly imagine she'd done it. I felt both proud of her and sick to my stomach. And terribly frightened for her. She was in a world of trouble.

Monday, I would have to terminate with her. But how could I do so when she was in such danger? She would no doubt think I was terminating with her so I could work with Ricardo. I would have to find a way to quickly terminate the work with him as well. I'd have to improvise, find a way to make him believe that ending our work was his idea.

I looked at my watch. Time to pick Allie up from school.

CHAPTER TWELVE

Allie and I sat across from each other, eating dinner at a small table in the kitchen. We'd taken to eating our meals there because to eat in the dining room reminded us too much of Claire's absence. I'd made Poke: ahi tuna marinated in soy sauce, ginger, and garlic, served over rice with avocado. I'd never made it when Claire was alive; by now, it had become one of Allie's favorites.

Allie texted off and on as she ate, which was fine with me because I was too distracted by the business with Ricardo and Angela to be very present to her. Ricardo would show up at my office on Monday, and earlier that same day I'd have to tell Angela I couldn't work with her anymore. Terminating with Angela went against every professional instinct I had, but I could think of no way around it.

Allie was still lost in her phone. We'd gone by Liz's house after school and explained the situation with Onesie. Allie had been so relieved at Liz's kind response, I realized she must have worried that Onesie's death might harm her relationship with her best friend. Maybe now was a good time to ask Allie why she hadn't left me a note when she'd gone out that morning. "Hey Allie," I said and waited for her to look up from her phone. When she did, her face was so open and innocent I considered letting the matter go. Did I really want to put at risk the fragile threads of connection that had grown between us since Onesie's death? Maybe, preoccupied with grief, she'd simply forgotten to write a note.

I tried to sound casual. "This morning when you left the house to walk to Biscayne Bay, did you think about leaving a note? So I wouldn't worry?"

A look of discomfort crossed Allie's face. "No," she said, but her denial was halting and tentative. I wasn't convinced.

I softened my voice. "Did you not think about it, or did you think about it, even for a second, and then decide not to?"

She stopped eating and looked down. "I guess so." I waited, leaving the ball in her court. She looked up. "When I got to the bay, I wished I *had* left a note."

The regret in her voice touched me. I thought about saying no more about the matter, except I knew regret needs an opening, a way out, or it can turn into a dark chord of self-hatred. I didn't want that for Allie. "You thought there was something wrong about not leaving a note?"

She angled her head to look at me. "'Course there was. It made you worry about me."

I shrugged my shoulders. "Maybe you wanted me to worry."

"Why, Daddy, *why* did I?" The admission was sudden and her question, her need to understand, endearing.

"Well, maybe you needed to let me know how hurt you were because Onesie escaping the house was partly my fault."

She shook her head. "I already told you it was my fault. I knew the garage door was open."

"Yes, but it shouldn't have been. I was careless to have left it open." I waited a beat. "Wasn't I?" I looked into her eyes and she did not look away.

She rested her chin on her hands. Her voice was barely audible. "I guess so."

"Allie, it's okay to be upset with me for leaving the garage door open. I'm upset with myself about it."

She sat up in the chair. "Are you upset with me, too, because I knew the garage door was open and I wasn't careful about it?"

I shook my head. "No, Allie, I'm not upset with you. You forgot, that's all."

She resumed eating her dinner, carefully pairing a wedge of avocado with each bite-size bit of tuna. After a minute or two, her phone pinged with a text message. I started to ask who it was but decided not to interrupt. As she sat pressing letters on the phone's keypad, a small smile lighting her face, I realized how isolated I had become. There was no one, apart from Allie, who could light my face like that. Roger hadn't reached out more than two or three times since Claire's death, and the one time we'd gotten together, he'd seemed uncomfortable and cut our time short. Gradually, I had withdrawn more and more into myself, creating a smaller, safer life.

Once a week, Claire's parents picked Allie up to take her out to dinner, but my interactions with them were perfunctory at best. My one life-giving connection to the world beyond Allie was my professional life—and it was now shredded by the way Ricardo had inserted himself into it. Instead of looking forward to a break on Monday from my seemingly fragile life with Allie, I was dreading the day.

I decided it would do me good to see a therapist myself. Maybe it would help me feel connected to *somebody*. I knew exactly who I wanted to work with: Dr. Walter Trogolo, a colleague who'd read a wonderful paper on grief at a conference I'd been to the year before. I excused myself from the table and went into my study to give him a call. I was in luck; Dr. Trogolo hadn't left the office. Though he didn't have any openings in his regular schedule, he offered to come in an hour early Monday morning to see a fellow therapist. I returned to the little table in the kitchen feeling lighter already.

After dinner, I read in the living room while Allie worked on homework in her bedroom. Now and then she came out and sat next to me on the sofa, once to show me a simple poem she'd written for her English class, another time to ask for my help in understanding fractions, then again to ask me to quiz her on the capital cities of various countries. Then at nine o'clock we watched a television show that had been a favorite before Claire died, one in which a young female reporter uncovers shady goings-on in business and politics, all the while giving ambiguous signals to the advances of a male photojournalist. The fact Allie wanted to watch the show together, and her reaching out for help with her homework, made me feel our connection was still strong. Stronger than I'd thought.

After the show, Allie got ready for bed. Once in bed she asked, as she had the night before, if I would bring her a glass of water. It pleased me to bring it to her. I was about to walk out of her bedroom when she spoke.

"Do you think we could ever get another kitten?"

"I suppose we could," I told her. She handed the empty glass to me and turned to face her rainbowed wall. I stayed awhile, watching Allie and the rainbow with the bluebird flying through its violet arc.

• • •

Early the next morning I lay in bed, somewhere between wakefulness and sleep. For an indeterminate amount of time I experienced the pleasant sensation of Claire in bed with me, one arm wrapped tightly around my chest. When I finally opened my eyes, I realized it was the top bedsheet that was wrapped around me, not Claire at all, and a hollowed-out feeling replaced the warmth and security I'd felt before.

Why had Claire visited me this morning? Did it have something to do with the loss of Onesie? Might Claire have visited Allie's bed as well? I rose and headed to Allie's room. It was Saturday and she had an early play-date with Liz.

She was still asleep, still facing the rainbowed wall, painted now with the soft light of early morning. I rested my hand on her shoulder. "Time to get up, Sweetpea." She rolled over, opened her eyes and looked at me without speaking. "What kind of bread do you want for your french toast?" I asked. "White or that awful rye you made me get?"

"Can I have cereal instead?" Her voice was faint, and flat.

In the kitchen, I watched as she prepared granola with milk and bananas. As she sat across from me with her mind in her cellphone, I wondered where the sweet girl from last night had gone, the one that asked me to bring her a glass of water. Somewhere over the rainbow, I supposed.

"You look unhappy," I said when she finally put her cellphone down.

She didn't have to say the words that were written all over her face and in the rolling of her eyes: *You're an idiot, Daddy.* And I was. I knew how grief works, how island moments of calm give way to hurt even graver than before. I, as much as anyone, knew that grief is a jealous lover, who cannot bear to have any part of you outside its grasp. Even though I knew these things, I didn't want them to be true for Allie.

"I'm sorry," I said. "That was a dumb thing to say."

Another roll of the eyes. I let her be and we spoke little the remainder of the morning or later, as I drove her to Liz's house. I thought she might ask again about a new kitten, or when we might get one, but she didn't. After she got out of the car, I waited and watched until the door of Liz's house closed behind her.

The rest of the day was mine. I hadn't the faintest idea what to do with it.

CHAPTER THIRTEEN

Monday morning. Time for my appointment with Dr. Trogolo. As can happen with many things, the purity of this event imagined from a distance became more ambiguous once it was close at hand. Would the doctor be able to help me, as I hoped, or might I be disappointed? And would I be able to cull from the jumble of thoughts crowding my mind a coherent narrative?

The office was simpler than I'd imagined. Like me, he had no receptionist, nor even a bell to let him know when I arrived. I supposed he would come out at my appointment time, eight o'clock. I'd been in therapy nearly two years during graduate school. It had been common practice back then to experience therapy from "the other side of the couch" if one wanted to join the profession. In that first course of therapy, I'd worked primarily on vulnerabilities to my self-esteem, the way I both needed attention yet rejected it. The therapy had helped, if for no other reason than it gave me a deeper empathy for myself. I'd been self-critical about my sensitivity to criticism, which is the very definition of a bind. I came to understand how I'd been a target for my father's shame, which he dealt with by projecting onto me qualities he despised in himself, then attacking me for them. During that initial foray into being a psychotherapy patient, I'd learned more than I'd known before about what a dangerous place the mind can be.

As the time for my appointment with Dr. Trogolo approached, I remembered a time when I was nine-years-old, waiting to perform at a piano recital. In spite of near immobilizing anxiety, I'd done fine. Now, the piece I would go on stage to play was one I hadn't sufficiently practiced, nor had any idea how to get through. The waiting room door opened and Dr. Trogolo came out to greet me. He was just as I remembered: a little man, probably in his fifties, with large brown eyes, thinning blond hair and an eager smile. Too eager. I felt a bit like I had to take care of the doctor by smiling back just as eagerly, when in fact I didn't feel like smiling at all.

When Dr. T. asked what I'd come in for, I realized how my own patients must feel: where to begin? With the accident that had taken Claire's life? Or with the dilemmas I faced in dealing with Ricardo. I started with Claire. It felt good to talk about her with someone whose job it was to understand the situation from *my* perspective, no one else's. This Dr. T. did well, wincing when I related Claire's words, "I'm seeing someone." It meant a lot that Dr. T.'s eyes held no judgement when I told him about missing the light turning yellow and then red. And when I told Dr. T. about the ensuing accident, he was at the edge of his seat, with me all the way. I only then fully appreciated how very alone I'd felt with all this pain.

I glanced at the clock. There were still fifteen minutes left. I told Dr. T there was something else I wanted to talk about. I told him about Ricardo, how the man had hijacked my work with Angela by threatening Allie and then wormed his way into my schedule by threatening me. When talking about Ricardo, I didn't use his real name. I called him "Roberto," just as Angela had.

I was just beginning to tell Dr. T. how I thought I'd have to terminate my work with Angela later that very morning when the doctor held up his hand. "Do you believe," he asked, his voice graver than before, "this man might actually carry out such threats?"

I told him I did, about how "Roberto" had orchestrated the murder of an undercover cop, and then about how he'd stabbed his driver and gotten away with it. I felt relieved to share these things. I was no longer so terribly alone with Ricardo's threats to my life and work.

Dr. T. frowned and sat up straighter in his chair. "Dr. Mason," he said, "I'm afraid you and I will not be able to work together."

I didn't understand. "Excuse me?"

"I am sorry, but I cannot take you on as a patient."

I thought, *haven't you already?* "Why not?" I asked.

"I suppose for the same reason you cannot work with your patient who is this man's girlfriend. Let me put it this way. You have said Roberto researched you, found out a great many things about you and about your daughter. If this is true, it is likely he will find out you are seeing me." Dr. T. paused meaningfully, as though it should be clear where he was headed.

It was not. "And…?"

"Suppose Roberto carries out one or more of these threats. Suppose he does something to harm his girlfriend, as you believe he wishes to do and is capable of doing. Suppose he harms you. Or, God forbid, your daughter."

I got it. "He would assume I would tell you about it, and you would then be a witness against him, which would put you in danger."

Dr. T. was nodding. "But," I continued, "you don't have any idea of his true identity."

"Roberto has no way of knowing this. So, as you say, if he were to carry out any of these threats, I would be in danger. Perhaps my family as well. I think you see my situation, do you not?"

I saw it all too well. It was like looking into a mirror.

CHAPTER FOURTEEN

Angela was running late for her appointment with Dr. Paul. Even so, she popped into the bathroom one last time to check her appearance. Not too bad, considering. She still had a bruise on her cheek where Ricardo had hit her and a bandage across her nose. She was looking forward to telling Dr. Paul how she'd bitten Ricardo's tongue and how she was free of him now—which was worth the beating she'd taken. She also planned to tell Dr. Paul how Michael had been harassed into leaving town, probably assaulted. Possibly killed. And though she was nervous about it, she would tell Dr. Paul about her father. It had never been her mind to do so, but she'd begun to think her father had been more important in her life than she'd realized.

She rang the bell in the waiting room and even before she had a chance to sit down, the door to Dr. Paul's office opened. By the look on his face, she wondered if Dr. Paul might be ill. If so, she could come back another time.

"I have something difficult to tell you," Dr. Paul said after she'd taken her seat. It looked like he was going to say more but then stopped himself. “What happened to your face?” he asked, a note of concern lighting his grey eyes.

“I had a fight with Ricardo. He went to kiss me and I…I bit off the tip of his tongue.” Angela had wondered whether Dr. Paul would be pleased or horrified by this news, but he didn’t seem to have any reaction at all, almost as though he already knew about it. “Ricardo was upset, very upset,” she continued. “He told me I was dead to him. He hasn’t contacted me since. I think I’m finally free of him.” Angela had expected to feel excited to share this news with Dr. Paul, had expected him to be excited too, but the look on his face was still grave. She remembered he’d said he had something difficult to tell her. She asked him what it was.

She didn’t understand what he said next, something about not working with her anymore. Was he taking a vacation? An early retirement? He spoke the same words again but they still made no sense, even though they echoed in her mind. *I can no longer work with you.* Unless…unless this was Ricardo’s doing. “Why?” she asked, hoping to find in his answer some room to bargain.

“I can’t be safe working with you. Nor can my daughter.” Dr. Paul looked pale, worse than before. More than his words, his expression told her this decision was not negotiable.

“Ricardo,” she said. Dr. Paul nodded his head and she felt herself sink beneath the raft of hope Dr. Paul had provided. This would be her last session. But…what if she presented Dr. Paul with an impossible choice? “Brian,” she said, her voice measured, “…my mother’s boyfriend…wasn’t the first.” Dr. Paul looked confused and started to say something, but she held her hand out to stop him. “When I was six,” she continued, a well of hurt so catching her by surprise she had to compose herself before going on—"When I was six, my father began touching me."

Dr. Paul looked off balance, a little upset even, but his voice was soft again. "Why are you telling me this?"

"Remember our first session?" she asked. "When I told you I didn't come here to talk about my father?" Dr. Paul nodded again. "Now I know…I have to." Dr. Paul looked…what was the word? *Forlorn.*

"Angela," he said, "I already told you I can't work with you anymore. Today has to be our last session."

"I still have forty minutes." She hesitated. It wasn't just that she didn't know how to start; she had an unexpected feeling that by telling Dr. Paul what had happened to her, she might infect him with her badness, just as her father had infected her with his. A silence stretched on until finally she closed her eyes and spoke, keeping her eyes shut the whole time. Everything she told Dr. Paul she could see in her mind and feel in her body.

• • •

Mami was spending the night with her sister, who'd just had a new baby, so Papi lay next to Angela in her parents' bed, reading to her from one of her nighttime storybooks. Papi had never done this before, read to her, and it confused her, but she liked the attention and so she moved closer, feeling the warmth of his body and secretly breathing in the smell of him. Where Mami smelled sugary-sweet, Papi was a different kind of sweet. Nearly sour. She put an arm around his chest and felt his breath rise and fall as he read the familiar story. Whenever Mami read the story, she made it come alive, her voice going soft and then loud and then soft again, but Papi read the story all in the same voice, so she paid attention not to the story, which she knew well anyway, but to the sound of him. It was, she thought, his private voice.

His body was so *big*. She stretched her arm out as far as she could and still wasn't able to reach to the other side of him. She felt a special kind of safety, lying next to him as he read to her in his low, rumbly voice. She wished he would look at her, like Mami did from time to time when she read, but he never did. She looked into his face and studied the whiskers stubbling from his cheeks, his nostrils full of hair, the black moustache that curled over the top of his upper lip.

Before she knew it, the story was over and he put the book down and elbowed himself up over her, her arm falling away from his chest. His enormous chocolate eyes shone down upon her. He was smiling and he spoke to her in a gentle, whispery voice, like he was saying a secret. "There's a way I can touch you that will show how special you are. Do you want me to do that?"

She did want to be special and she said so, but the way he touched her felt both good and bad at the same time. She tried to relax and learn about this new thing as he snuggled his face into her neck and gave her little kisses while continuing to touch her down there. After a minute or two he let out a sound like he might be hurt and it scared her, so even though he was touching her too hard and she wanted him to stop, she didn't say anything. Instead, she closed her eyes and thought about sitting on Pietra's porch as Pietra rocked quietly and told stories about when *she* was little girl. Pietra, with her white hair and brown eyes so deep with knowing. She thought about the time Pietra sent her down to the corner bodega to buy a Coca-Cola. It was hot out but had just rained, so it wasn't as hot as before. Inside the concrete-block bodega, an old man with bushy black hair opened a bottle of Coca-Cola, its thick green glass dull with condensation. She gave him the coins Pietra had given her and took the bottle from the man, holding it where it was narrow in the middle, a thing nearly perfect in her hand. She poured a little of the dark liquid into her mouth, savoring the cold, fizzy thrill of it. When she turned to go back outside, the fabric of her skirt caught the air and lifted into a rippling wave of blue.

• • •

Angela opened her eyes. It took her a moment to realize where she was—no longer in the bodega on her way back to Pietra with a cool Coca-Cola in her hand, no longer in bed with Papi, wishing she were somewhere else, but in Dr. Paul's office, his eyes wet with tears.

"I'm so sorry, Angela" Dr. Paul said. As though he had been the one to hurt her.

She didn't know what to say. She wanted him to sit beside her and wrap his arms around her and at the same time she didn't want that. She rested in the kindness of his eyes, and it was as though the two of them were holding the hurt little girl she'd told him about.

He looked at the clock on the table beside her. She knew what that meant, and as she stood to leave his office she hoped that after she'd told him about her father, Dr. Paul would have to keep her. She was waiting for the words to come, about scheduling her next appointment.

"Wait a minute," he said. "There's something you should know."

She stood still and waited, thinking here they come, the words she'd hoped for.

"You should know I'm going to have to start working with Ricardo. I don't really want to, but he's made me an offer I can't refuse." Dr. Paul looked at her meaningfully.

Angela felt dizzy and thought she might need to return to her chair. Of course, Ricardo could pay twice, three times, ten times her fee. Feeling deeply betrayed, she didn't know what to do but turn and walk out of the room. Just before she reached the door, her eyes already blurred with tears, Dr. Paul said he had one more thing to tell her. In exchange for working with Ricardo, he'd gotten Ricardo to promise to let her go. Apparently, Dr. Paul hadn't heard her say she was already free of Ricardo.

She left Dr. Paul's office feeling abandoned by the one person she'd thought might help her—and not at all sure what she would do with the freedom she now had.

CHAPTER FIFTEEN

I wanted time itself to stop. It had already been an impossible day. My attempt to get help for myself had left me feeling abandoned and betrayed, with all hope of finding relief from my isolation gone. Now Angela had made my job of terminating with her that much harder by telling me what had happened with her father. It hurt me to think about it. There was nothing right about terminating with her.

After several intervening patients and a lunch break, my three o'clock appointment with Ricardo was at hand. I walked reluctantly to the door of my waiting room, feeling as though I was about to invite a malevolent force into my office. Into my life. My only hope was to find a way to work with the man as short a time as possible and then cut him loose. His threat to break my legs in several places hadn't been far from my mind since the threat had first been made—or the "joke," as Ricardo later called it.

When I opened the door and saw Ricardo sitting there in his expensive, three-piece suit, I felt sick not just physically but in my soul. Pushing against everything inside me that wanted Ricardo far away, I invited the man into my office. Smiling, he sat across from me, his black eyes showing no indication of unease.

"Tell me again why you are here," I said.

"I am here for therapy, of course."

Ricardo seemed to think he'd answered my question. I asked him what he wished to accomplish in therapy.

"I told you." Ricardo opened his mouth, showed me his severed tongue, waggled it back and forth. "Angela should be suffering now. Beyond suffering. Yet I cannot bring myself to hurt her. Or have her hurt."

"Can you say more about that?" I asked, going through the motions, not really interested in Ricardo's answer.

Ricardo shifted in his chair. "I do not know what you mean."

"Let me put it differently. How is it that you have come to define yourself in this way—as one who must give an eye for an eye."

"I told you before. I do not give an eye for an eye. You take one eye, I take two."

"Because…?"

Ricardo looked flustered. "Is it not obvious? One must avenge an attack."

"And yet with Angela, you can't avenge. Why not?"

Ricardo spoke impatiently, as though I were asking him to repeat what he'd already said. "You know the answer to this. Because I care about her in a way I did not know it was possible to care."

I harnessed my own impatience, worked to keep my voice neutral. "You are telling me that you care more about Angela, as a person, than you do about avenging her attack. Is that right?"

"I had not thought about it that way, but yes."

"And what is that like for you?"

Ricardo straightened in his chair. "It is something terrible. It means I have become a weak man."

I spoke softly, beginning to be more engaged. "Are you, Ricardo? A weak man?"

Ricardo curled his lip. "I am not." He said this aggressively, as though I had accused him of such.

"I didn't think so," I said. "It is possible, then, to be a strong man, and yet care so much about someone you don't want to hurt them. Even if they have hurt you. Yes?"

For the first time in the session, Ricardo looked thoughtful. "It is possible. A strong man has many choices." His voice picked up volume. "But is it desirable?"

"Is it, Ricardo?"

"*No.*"

"And why not?"

"Because it sends a message that one can be taken advantage of."

We were going in circles now. How to find a soft spot? Surely Ricardo had one. Everyone does. I waited to see if he would say more, but the silence between us lengthened uncomfortably. Some patients welcome silence, use it as one might use a front-porch rocker on a fine summer afternoon: to go inward, to reflect. Ricardo was not such a person. I remembered what Angela had told me about Ricardo's childhood. I asked him, "How did you come to be so concerned about...*justice?*" Ricardo looked confused, so I elaborated. "You know, an eye for an eye."

"Ah, yes, the history. This is what you want now."

Ricardo's tone was irritating. He'd obviously come with a well-rehearsed "history," which he would use not as an opening into vulnerability but just the opposite, as a defense. I wanted none of it.

"No, Ricardo," I said. "I don't want 'the history.'" I leaned forward and held eye contact with the man. "A minute ago, you said it makes you feel weak that you can't exact revenge on Angela. When was the last time, previous to this, that you felt weak?"

Ricardo's eyes grew fractionally larger, and for the first time in the session he looked truly off balance. Then, as though a curtain had been drawn, he regained his composure. "I do not know what you mean."

"I think you do know what I mean. I saw it in your face. Look, I don't ask this question to get an upper hand." Though I knew I must have the upper hand to get anywhere with him. "I ask it to help you connect to a part of yourself you might have buried. The parts of ourselves we bury exert control over us." Ricardo was looking at me intently. "I think you don't want to be controlled. Am I right?"

Ricardo didn't move at all.

"Ricardo, when was the last time, before now, you felt weak?" When he didn't respond, I added, "Helpless."

Ricardo gave me a look so venomous I thought he might actually attack me. Then he stood and walked out the door.

I let out a breath and looked at the clock. Less than fifteen minutes had passed. I'd been too abrupt, of course. Unless they're in a crisis, patients don't like to reveal such vulnerable aspects of themselves in the first session. But Ricardo had been trying to control the session and I wasn't going to let him get away with it. There was more than that, though, and it wasn't pretty to admit: I wanted to defeat the man more than I wanted to help him. How could I work effectively with such a despicable motivation? Well, it didn't matter. Ricardo wouldn't be back, not after I'd shown him where this therapy was headed. Like Angela, I was free of him now.

The rest of the day went by like most workdays: periods of agonizing dullness alternating with sublime and surprising intimacies. In one session, a patient too frightened to reveal anything real talked on and on about the most efficient way to organize a trip through the grocery store. The clock that measured the progress of time seemed stuck in quicksand. In the very next session, time disappeared altogether as I became immersed in a long-term patient's riveting struggle to overcome a lifetime of mistrust by risking, for the first time, real intimacy with a man. "I've never been in this place with a man before," Lucy said, leaning forward so she was sitting at the very front of her chair. "Maybe I should end it now, before he finds out who I really am."

"Do you want to?" I asked.

Lucy took a deep breath, then sat back in the chair. "No. But I don't know if I can stand to be this scared."

"Can you stand it one more day?"

She smiled ruefully. "I guess so."

I drove home feeling wholly wrung out. I couldn't remember a more emotionally exhausting workday: the failure of my own therapy, the difficult termination with Angela, the session with Ricardo. And what would I face at home? Onesie's death had set Allie back in a big way. After I'd picked her up at Liz's house on Saturday, she'd been morose all weekend. The worst part was the way she'd kept to herself, not wanting my help in any way. My own grief I could handle. Watching hers was nearly unbearable.

When I opened the door, Allie was on the couch with the television on, studying something on a table in front of her. Sarah sat next to her, helping her with whatever they were working on. Allie looked up but didn't smile. "Hello, Allie," I said, trying to make my voice sound pleasant, but not too pleasant. Not false.

"Hi," she replied, her tone serious. She didn't look happy to see me. I knew I shouldn't take it personally, but I wasn't in such good shape myself. I retreated to the kitchen to fix myself a drink. After Sarah left, Allie came in and stood for a bit without speaking. I was about to ask what was on her mind when she moved closer. "Can we maybe look for another kitten today? Sarah said there are websites where you can adopt kittens who don't have a home."

I was relieved. She was asking for my help, and this was something I could actually do. Even better, we would do it together. I retrieved the laptop from my briefcase and we sat side-by-side on the sofa, going through one kitten after another. After twenty minutes, Allie hadn't found any she liked. I was about to suggest we look at another website when she asked, "Can we get a *new* kitten?"

"I've got some time tomorrow," I said. "We'll go to the pet store at the mall. Maybe they'll have some kittens for us to look at."

The next afternoon we went to the pet store. There was one kitten available, entirely black except for her greenish orange eyes. When Allie pressed her face close to its cage and called to it, the kitten pranced up and fitted its little paw between the bars of the cage to touch her face. Allie looked up at me. "I like this one. Can we take her home?"

On the ride back, with the new kitten stretched across Allie's lap like a tiny black blanket, I asked if she'd decided on a name.

"I'm going to call her Twosome."

CHAPTER SIXTEEN

Two days later, with an hour free between patients, I made a last-minute decision to grab a snack from a deli down the street. As I was about to open the door to the waiting room, the bell rang indicating a patient's arrival. I checked my watch. I wasn't expecting anyone. I opened the door and a thread of electricity ran through me. There sat Ricardo Raphael, wearing a charcoal grey, three-piece suit and smiling politely, as though what had happened between us three days ago had not occurred.

Noting my surprise, Ricardo consulted his Rolex. "Is it not time for our session, Dr. Mason? Did you not say we would meet twice a week, Mondays and Thursdays, at three?"

"I didn't expect you back," I said, as weakly as I felt.

"Did I call to cancel, Dr. Mason?" He took a couple of steps toward me, too close. "If I had decided to discontinue therapy, I would have called to let you know. I do not like to be left hanging, so I try not to do it to others." He walked past me into the office and took a seat.

I followed him in, disbelieving he had actually returned and wishing I could be anywhere else. I searched through fragmented thoughts to recall the details of our previous session. I had to figure out how best to proceed, and this time I wanted to keep a tight rein on my motivation. Defeating Ricardo, even if I could do it, wasn't worth the cost to my professional self-esteem. I looked him in the eye. "When you walked out the other day, did you know you'd be back?" There was an uncharacteristic harshness to my voice, but the question was a good one. And fair.

Ricardo turned his head to one side, less composed than before. "I did not know, but I thought so, yes."

The next obvious question: "What was going through your mind when you walked out?"

Ricardo looked down for a beat before returning his eyes to me. "I had…an unpleasant memory. It surprised me. I was…caught off guard."

I leaned forward. "And the memory…?"

Ricardo stood and I thought he might leave again, but instead he began to walk back and forth in the small office, his hands in the pockets of his pants. "I knew you would ask this, so I prepared myself. I went through the memory before coming here, saying it out loud. Of course, it is different saying it to another person." He stopped pacing, looked at me. I was struck that he'd taken the time to prepare. He started to pace again. "Before my mother was shot by the Colombian army, one of the bastards…" Ricardo stopped pacing and shook his head before continuing. "One of the bastards raped her. They tried to make me watch, but my mother told me to close my eyes and place my hands over my ears. I did so, and when I opened my eyes again, she was gone." Ricardo looked toward the window of my office, his voice barely audible. "I never saw her again."

Ricardo seemed human now, and what was happening between us felt like real therapy. "What you've told me," I said, "…the word *horrific* comes to mind." I let this sink in as Ricardo watched me closely. "How old were you?"

Ricardo returned to his chair. "I was twelve."

I let a moment pass, then lowered my voice. "What was it like for you to experience this as a twelve-year-old boy?"

Ricardo's eyes hardened. "You go, as they say, for the jugular."

"I'm not trying to harm you." I hoped this was true.

There was a rising anger in Ricardo's voice. "You are trying—*what*—then?"

"If I'm to help you, I need to understand what has shaped you."

Ricardo's voice carried an unexpected note of triumph. "You have helped me already, Dr. Mason."

"I've helped you? How?"

"Remember what I came here for?"

My stomach tightened. "You said you came because you thought Angela should suffer, but you couldn't bring yourself to do it."

"You have an excellent memory. Even though I do not see you taking notes."

"I make notes after the session." I crossed one leg over the other. "What do you mean I've helped you already?" It was a question I wasn't sure I wanted the answer to.

Ricardo's face seemed to age in the matter of a few seconds. "Do you have any idea," he said, "what I've been through these past few days? Since I remembered my mother being raped?"

"Tell me," I said.

"I will *not* tell you." Ricardo spit out the words. "You are one greedy bastard. Greedy to feast on the weakness of others. *On all the little details*." He paused, took a mouthful of water from a plastic cup he'd brought in from the waiting room, put the cup back on the table. "And you think *I* am the monster." He sat back, saying nothing more.

I considered waiting him out, but I figured Ricardo would wait the entire session if need be. "We've gotten sidetracked," I said. "You were telling me how I've helped you."

Ricardo sat slightly forward again. "After I left your office the other day and was forced to relive this incident with my mother, I came to see how soft I have become. Too soft. I had then what you would call an insight." He waited for me to ask the inevitable question.

"What was your insight?"

Ricardo's eyes were cold now, with no humanity in them at all. "I realized how foolish it is to let anyone gain the upper hand. *Anyone*. Even someone you have come to care about."

My stomach tightened again. "You mean Angela."

"Yes. My *Angelina*. I have what I need now to overcome my weakness where she is concerned."

"You see love as a weakness?"

"Oh, no. Love is a beautiful thing. And it does not have to make one weak. You have taught me this. If a man stays connected to his roots, he can love and still be strong. Strong enough to do what needs to be done."

I was afraid to ask the next obvious question. "What does it mean for you to be strong in the face of your love for Angela?"

"It means," Ricardo said, sitting ramrod straight, "I will take my revenge." He let a moment pass. "And this will not diminish my love for her at all."

Nausea was turning my stomach. I glanced at the trash can by my desk in case I might need it. "Ricardo," I said, "if you are coming here simply to get to the point where you can harm Angela, I cannot work with you."

Ricardo looked incredulous. "Dr. Mason, at no time have I made any pretense about why I am here. If you did not believe me, if you did not trust me, that is on you."

"No matter. I will not work with you under these conditions." It felt good to be so clear.

Ricardo smiled. "Have you forgotten about the matter of my fee?"

I looked again at the trash can, tried to give my words a strength I did not feel. "You said you were joking."

"Is it not true, Dr. Mason, that in certain situations, coercion works best if it is concealed? If the gun is in the open, one cannot forget it is there. But if the gun is...hidden...might it not be forgotten? Wished away, perhaps."

My mind froze. I hadn't forgotten his threat, but I had wished it away. It took nearly a minute before I could speak again and when I did, the venom in my voice surprised me. "Is this how you played it with Angela, too? You pretended you were in a real relationship, that you weren't *raping* her?" I was no therapist now. I knew that.

There was a smirk on Ricardo's face, the man undoubtedly enjoying my unraveling, and I knew I had to somehow unplug from my gut. Perhaps the only way forward under these circumstances was to do my best to be a therapist. Angela had probably made the same decision: to be the best companion and lover she could be, acting as if she'd not been compelled to do so.

"Ricardo," I said, "exactly what do you plan to do to Angela?"

Ricardo relaxed in the chair. "Remember, Dr. Mason, when I said I give not an eye for an eye, but *two* eyes?"

The ball of dread tightened in my stomach. "I remember."

"Angela bit off the tip of my tongue, did she not?"

I waited for him to continue.

"So. I will take Angela's tongue and cut the whole of it out." Ricardo studied his fingernails a moment before looking at me again. "Do you know, Dr. Mason, that a human tongue, in its entirety, is surprisingly long?"

I held his eyes and did not speak. What was there to say?

"And after I cut out her tongue, I will come to our next session and tell you exactly what it was like to do so. This is what you insist upon, is it not? *All the little details?*"

I didn't doubt Ricardo would do exactly that, and for the first time in my professional life I felt entirely defeated. For many moments Ricardo and I sat in silence, Ricardo calm now, waiting. Waiting for what, I had no idea. Finally, he said, "You are good, Dr. Mason. Very good. I expected you to argue with me about this."

It struck me that the impotence and rage I now felt must mirror what Ricardo felt as a twelve-year-old boy watching his mother get raped. This ability of patients to re-create within the therapist their own deep dynamics never failed to impress me. "I think when we suffer a violent attack," I said, hoping to show Ricardo how well I understood him, "…it is natural to want to destroy the offending party. To obliterate them."

A thoughtful look crossed Ricardo's face. "So, Dr. Mason. Do you wish to destroy *me?*"

It took me aback, how completely Ricardo understood my state of mind. "I might," I admitted. This was not the time nor place for lies.

Ricardo's voice was soft. "So, you and I, we are not so different."

"I didn't say I would. I said I *might*." I knew I was being defensive.

Ricardo rose and stood over me, his voice softer still. "Here is another question for you, Dr. Mason." He waited, letting the moment build. "Is this therapy moving in the direction of making *me* more like *you?* Or is it perhaps moving in quite the opposite direction?" He turned and walked out of the office.

I closed my eyes and took several deep breaths, trying to settle. Ricardo was probably right. I had been changed by our work more than he. My next thought was that I had to warn Angela. Ricardo hadn't simply played out a fantasy, he'd expressed intent. But if I were to warn Angela or notify the police, what would Ricardo do? To Angela? To me? To Allie?

I looked at the clock. Again, Ricardo hadn't been able to tolerate an entire forty-five minutes. Yet I had no doubt that in four days, he would be back for his next appointment. By that time, would he have taken his revenge on Angela?

Would I have to hear "all the little details?"

CHAPTER SEVENTEEN

During the next two hours I functioned on autopilot, unable to connect deeply with either of my patients. When it came time to leave, I called my friend and colleague Roger to ask if he'd ever been in a situation like this or ever heard of one. Roger said he hadn't. I shared my dilemma about warning Angela. "I have to, legally, but if I do, what if it pisses the man off and he comes after me? Or Allie?"

Roger sympathized but insisted I had to find some way to warn my patient. "If your guy carries out the threat and you haven't warned his girlfriend, what will that do to you?" I understood what Roger was getting at, but I also knew what it would do to me if I warned Angela and Ricardo came after Allie.

I arrived home completely spent. When I opened the front door, Twosome bolted from the couch and ran into Allie's bedroom. Allie came out with the kitten in her arms, Sarah following close behind. "Twosome's not used to you yet," Allie said. She offered the kitten for me to hold, but twice before when I'd tried to hold her, the cat had mewed and struggled hard to get away, scratching me in the process. I declined Allie's offer. She put the kitten on the floor, where it rubbed itself back and forth against her leg.

"How was your day at the office?" Sarah asked.

How could I explain the expertly crafted vise Ricardo had placed me in? "The usual," I lied. "My job is sort of like an airline pilot's. Hours of boredom interspersed with moments of sheer panic." Sarah laughed and gathered her things to leave. After she was gone, Allie asked what we were having for dinner. I didn't have the energy to cook and suggested we go out.

"But this is only our third night with Twosome," Allie said. "I don't want to leave her."

I was in even less of a mood to argue than to cook, so I gave in. "How about hot dogs," I said. "With potato chips and fresh fruit for dessert?" Allie liked a lot of ketchup on her dogs, and didn't ketchup count as a vegetable these days?

"Not hot dogs, Daddy. Pork chops. On the grill, with rice and peas. I already looked. We have some in the freezer."

How could I say no? How could I deny her anything? These moments of near normalcy between us were all I had left.

While the pork chops thawed under tap water, I sat in the large recliner in the living room. I was too wound up to watch television or look at my phone, so I closed my eyes and tried to rid my mind of all thought. After a few minutes, Allie came into the room. "Wanna start a game of Monopoly?" she asked. "I already did my homework." She must have seen my hesitation because she said, "*Please?*" She'd fallen in love with the game in the past month or so, had even downloaded a tip sheet from the Internet. Several times, I'd noticed her studying it.

"Okay. Let me get supper together. Then we can play."

After dinner, I sat across from her on the floor of her room while she rolled the dice across the Monopoly board. For her, it was all about the game, how to take advantage of what luck brought—which properties to buy and which to pass up. For me, it was all about time with her. As she moved her tiny silver dog down the board, lightly touching each square she passed, I wondered if I'd be playing this game with Allie if Claire were still alive. Probably not; I would have considered it a waste of too much time, especially on a workday. And if Claire were here, would Allie have taken up the game? No telling. A longing for Claire welled within me; I wished she were lying next to us on the bed, knitting while we played.

Allie's roll of the dice landed her on a question mark and she drew a card that sent her directly to jail. "Can you believe that?" she asked, her voice ringing with exasperation. As though this were a real hardship.

"You're having bad luck this time," I said. Earlier, I'd landed on Park Place and bought it. I already had Boardwalk and by now I'd established two houses on it. I took my turn, passed GO and collected $200. Allie, still incarcerated, glared at me. Twosome pranced into the room, and when Allie rolled the dice trying for doubles to get out of jail, the kitten jumped onto the board, catching one of the dice between her paws. As Twosome slid across the surface of the board, she sent my little houses and Allie's silver dog skittering across the carpet. The kitten flicked the captured die with her paw and chased it across the room.

Allie laughed so hard she fell over backward. When she sat up again, she gathered Twosome into her lap. The kitten mewed and squirmed, as if to say she was in the middle of some serious hunting, if you please. I envied Allie's ability to fully enter the moment.

I was both there and not there, part of me still feeling the grip of Ricardo's vise.

"Let's not finish the game, okay?" Allie said. "You were going to beat me anyway."

"I don't know about that, Allie. You're pretty good at playing the long game."

Allie, still holding Twosome in her lap, looked at me with puzzlement. "What's 'the long game'?"

"You know the expression, 'in the short run?'"

"Yeah."

"Well, to play the long game is just the opposite. It means looking at things from the perspective of a long time. In the case of Monopoly, it means regarding the game as a whole, not for only one or two moves."

"You mean like, in the long game, we're gonna have to leave planet Earth and find another place to live?"

I'd been picking up game pieces from the floor and stopped to look at her. "That's a *really* long game."

"But it's true, isn't it? If we're gonna survive, we have to find some other place." When I didn't respond, she added, "You don't like to think about it, do you?" She set Twosome down and began to help pick up the rest of the Monopoly pieces. Together we put all the pieces in the box and Allie put the box back in its place on the top shelf of a small bookcase in her bedroom.

I sat on her bed and invited her to join me. "You're right," I said. "I don't like to think about the world coming to an end."

"It's disturbing," she said. I couldn't remember her ever using that word before, and it touched me to hear her say it. It was just the right word.

After a moment, as we sat quietly on the bed, I asked, "Are there other things you worry about?"

"Well, I found out we're gonna have to leave the planet long before the sun burns out."

This surprised me; I'd expected her to turn to more earthly concerns. Although I supposed this *was* an "earthly" concern. "Why is that?" I asked, though I thought I knew the answer.

"For us to be here, the temperature has to be just right. Not too hot and not too cold. At some point, it's gonna get too hot or too cold, even with the sun still around." She looked at me as a teacher might address a student. "The temperature has been just right for only a short period of time. Only the last few hundred million years."

"Allie, where did you learn this?"

"On the internet. I've been researching what it takes for life to happen."

"You haven't told me about that."

"You don't want to know."

"You're right," I said, putting a note of apology in my voice. "But I do want to know what worries you."

She looked down at her feet and a sadness came over her. Was it about Claire? Did she, too, sense whispers of her mother still present in the house? Allie lay back on the bed and looked at me. Like a cat, now, inscrutable. So much like Claire it comforted and hurt me at the same time. I attempted a smile, hoping to get her to reveal what she was thinking. But even at nine years old, something in her was stronger than me just now. Probably, it was that I needed her approval too much. Down deep, it was what I wanted more than anything. I looked away.

"Daddy?" Allie's voice seemed older than her years.

I didn't look back. "Yes, Allie?"

"You look sad."

I didn't want to get into it with her, the grief thing, even though I'd been wondering if she felt it too.

"Is it about Mommy?"

"Yes, it's partly about your mother. I miss her sometimes. But I'm also sad because I thought you were sad."

"It came on sudden—you know?" She lay down on the bed and I thought I saw a tear leak out the corner of one eye. I tried to lie next to her, but she rolled further away. "There's something else," she said, eyes closed, her voice full of a feeling I couldn't decipher. I waited for her to elaborate. When she didn't, I asked her what it was.

"Something hard to talk about." Her eyes were still closed.

I wanted to let her know she could tell me anything and it would be okay, but the clinician in me advised to follow the resistance. "What makes it hard?"

She was quiet for what seemed like a long stretch of time. Surely more than a minute. "It's about you." She took a pillow from the bed and held it against her chest. "You…" I couldn't make out the rest of what she said because she said it into the pillow, her voice muffled. But I heard the last word, "road," and I thought I knew what she meant. I'd taken my eyes off the road. She took the pillow away and looked at me, her eyes blurred, then fell back on the bed, sobbing so hard I worried she might suffocate. I wanted to hold her in my arms, but I knew she wouldn't allow that right now.

I thought I'd managed to escape the landmine of Allie blaming me for Claire's death. We'd spoken about it and put it behind us. But I knew better. I knew when deep feelings are brushed aside, they return with greater force. The only thing to do was sit there, hoping an opening might develop between us.

Eventually, Allie's sobbing subsided. She sat up and faced me again, giving me a long look before speaking. "Daddy, what made you do it?"

There was no good answer.

"You said Mommy told you she was unhappy."

"Yes."

"Do you know what she was unhappy about? Do you have any idea?"

Dangerous ground. How much of the truth to tell? "I thought maybe she was unhappy with me," I finally said. "That's why it grabbed my attention the way it did."

"What about you?"

"Allie, I wish I knew. I would give anything to know."

Allie seemed to sink into the bed. She shook her head ever so slightly and when she spoke again, she told me she needed to get ready for bed. She said it nicely, politely, but the words cut. She was dismissing me. I left the room but didn't close the door. I went to the big chair in the living room where, after a while, I heard her get up, then saw her walk to the bathroom. The sound of running water let me know she was brushing her teeth, washing her face. I wondered if she would come by and tell me goodnight, or once in bed ask me to bring her a glass of water as she'd done nearly every night since that first time. But after a minute or two she returned to her bedroom and closed the door. After another minute, the light under the door went dark. I sat for a long time, unable to rise from the weight of a regret I believed I would carry the rest of my life.

Eventually something bubbled up through my pain. I had a decision to make, what to do about Angela. I was legally and ethically bound to warn her. But if I deprived Ricardo of the opportunity to take his revenge, he might want to punish me instead. Getting to Allie would be the best way to do that.

I picked up the phone and pressed the small blue string of numbers that appeared in my contact list below Angela's name. After a few rings, she picked up.

"Dr. Paul?"

"Hello, Angela." My voice sounded lifeless as a recording.

"Why are you calling?"

"I have a legal and ethical obligation to tell you that Ricardo has threatened to harm you. I think he's serious. I hope you will take steps to protect yourself."

"I have a gun. I've been to the range and I know how to use it."

I didn't think having a gun would be enough to keep her safe, but I'd given my warning. Without thinking, I asked her how she was doing.

There was no response.

"Have you found someone else to work with?"

She had closed the connection.

CHAPTER EIGHTEEN

It was nearly time for Ricardo Raphael's appointment. The dread that had parked in the back of my stomach all weekend now moved into my chest. When I opened the door to the waiting room, would I know just by looking at the man whether he'd carried out his threat against Angela?

I braced myself and opened the door.

Ricardo wasn't there. Of course. There'd been no bell to indicate his arrival. Flush with relief, I sat in one of the waiting room chairs trying to think what this might mean. Had Ricardo hurt Angela but didn't want to put himself in legal jeopardy by talking about it? Was he through with therapy after all? I pulled out my cell to call Angela to make sure she was okay, but before I could do so Ricardo came bustling through the outer door. It hadn't occurred to me he might simply be late.

"I am sorry, Dr. Mason. I was caught in traffic behind an accident just outside your office. I was going to call to let you know, but then the traffic cleared. I thought I might be able to make it on time." He looked at his watch. "Ahh…close, but not quite. Again, I apologize."

What a hypocrite, I thought. The man pretended to be civilized but wouldn't hesitate to have my legs broken at the snap of a finger. "Come in," I said with a sigh. I hadn't seen on Ricardo's face or heard anything in his voice that indicated his state of mind—or Angela's fate.

Even before I settled into my chair, Ricardo said, "I think you will be pleased with what I have to tell you." I thought the only thing that would please me would be if Ricardo were to say he'd decided to terminate our work together. Or even better, commit suicide. "I have decided," he continued, "not to harm Angela. Not yet, anyway." Ricardo waited for me to respond. When I didn't, he asked, "Don't you want to hear about it?" I continued looking at him, not wanting to give him the courtesy of a response, though I was interested in hearing what he had to say. Ricardo brushed lint from one leg of his pants. "I was going to do it. Do it myself, not have one of my people do it for me. The tongue, as we discussed."

Like hell, we discussed. Don't act like this was a jointly crafted plan.

"But then I thought about how I would feel after. Not right after, when I would feel gloriously avenged, but how I would feel the following week, or month, or six months after."

Ricardo waited for me to play my part. I just stared at him. But I was impressed with what he'd said.

"I realized I would regret that I did not give her another chance to do the right thing."

I was sufficiently struck by the depth of Ricardo's thinking that I wanted to hear more. "What is the 'right thing' you would have her do?"

"Come back to me, of course. I miss her terribly. Even though she bit off part of my tongue, I miss her. Is that not true love, Dr.

Mason? And does she not owe me this, to come back—after I decided not to hurt her?"

Do you really want Angela to be with you out of obligation, rather than desire? I thought this, but what I said was, "I think what you've told me today is important. You've learned to look ahead—to consider the outcome of an impulsive wish."

Ricardo smiled a wide smile, showing his immaculate teeth. "I told you that you would be pleased."

"Why don't we take a break then?" It was a shot in the dark. "It will give you some time to build on this accomplishment." Of course, to quit now made no sense. Ricardo was at a critical turning point. If he were a real patient, it would be important to continue our work. With a sick feeling, I remembered Ricardo's closing statement the previous session. "*Is this therapy moving in the direction of making me more like you? Or is it perhaps moving in quite the opposite direction?*" I had to admit my suggestion that Ricardo take a break was entirely self-serving.

"Actually, Dr. Mason," Ricardo said, "I was planning to propose the same thing. But there is one more thing I want to tell you."

"Yes?"

"When I realized the *thought* of hurting Angela would be far more pleasurable than the thing itself, I saw something else." His expression turned more serious. "I have lived my entire life with a hatred of the man who raped my mother, who undoubtedly killed her. I have wanted to extract my revenge on this man." Ricardo stopped talking to let out a long breath. "I realize I cannot avenge his barbaric acts. I do not even know this man. More than likely, he is dead now."

I was stunned. I hadn't thought Ricardo capable of such insight. Feeling a quiet excitement for the first time in our work together, I said, "You realized that if you did to Angela what you said you would do, you would be exacting revenge on the wrong person."

"Yes." After a moment, Ricardo added, "But...she did bite off my tongue."

"*Why*, Ricardo? Why did she do that?"

Ricardo's pupils grew wide. "Because she felt as I have felt—the need to extract something." He closed his eyes. "A revenge."

This was no well-rehearsed performance. Ricardo was working hard to understand something, to get to the other side of it, where his life might be different than it had been before. I spoke softly. "You know something about that, don't you Ricardo. The desire for revenge." Ricardo looked down at his feet, then up again. I let a moment pass. "So, we take a break now? In the work?" In saying this I was betraying everything I believed in, betraying the very profession to which I'd devoted my entire adult life. Ricardo was making real progress. But I couldn't stand the thought of sitting with him another minute, much less for the hours and weeks and years it would take for therapy to make a lasting difference.

"Yes, Dr. Mason. We can take a break. I will call you when I want to come in again."

A weight of tension I hadn't realized I'd been carrying left me. I rose from my chair and waited for him to do the same. Ricardo took out his wallet, counted out bills and handed them to me. I took the money, stuffed it into my pocket, then walked to the door that led into the waiting room and opened it.

As I closed the door behind Ricardo, I felt emptied of everything that mattered to me, except Allie. I closed my eyes and thought of her, how after the aborted Monopoly game she'd shut me out. Since then I'd hardly seen her. Liz had invited several girls over for a sleepover Saturday night and Allie arranged to spend Friday night with her as well, "to help Liz get ready." She hadn't come home until Sunday afternoon. She'd been friendly then, but cool, preferring to eat supper by herself in her room, "catching up on homework."

I walked back to the chair beside my desk, where for the next three hours I listened to the heartaches and heartbreaks of a trio of souls. In between appointments I thought about Angela. I thought her life must seem entirely hopeless now, having been failed by the one profession that should have offered promise. Having been failed by the one person who *had* offered promise.

At the end of the day, as I sat in my chair trying to summon the energy to return to a home broken possibly beyond repair, I had a thought I'd never had before, nor even imagined I might have.

I've got to find another line of work.

PART TWO

CHAPTER NINETEEN

Six Years Later

A sudden movement of the ship awakened me earlier than I would have liked. For unknown minutes I slipped in and out of a light sleep, savoring both the lingering anesthesia in my limbs and the gently rolling movements of the ship upon the water. I loved these mornings, the feeling of being gently rocked. Eventually I stretched, got out of bed and walked across the small space between my bed and the tiny window of my cabin. Just above the horizon, thin bands of crimson held the promise of sunrise. I wished I could open the window and smell the salted air.

I set coffee to brewing and sat in a chair by the window, where last evening I'd spent long hours reading and, not for the first time, drinking too much Scotch. While the coffee hissed to life, I opened the calendar on my phone. Today's schedule was unusually robust: three obviously married couples—same last name—followed by two in the afternoon whose different last names conveyed an uncertain legal status, and at the end of the day an individual female. I hoped this woman would not be like one from yesterday who, recovering from a divorce, had used the session to try to seduce me.

In the second year following Claire's death I'd tried online dating—once. The entire evening I'd been preoccupied with the many ways this woman, Susan, was not Claire. When Susan smiled, she was all in. When Claire smiled, she held something back—as though she were having a conversation with herself about the smile. I fell in love with the mystery of Claire, with the challenge she presented. On the rare occasions I was able to draw her out, or more likely when she allowed me to, the connection between us had been unlike anything I'd ever experienced.

After that one attempt at dating I resolved to learn to live alone, and in this I'd been perhaps too successful. If not exactly happy, my life the last handful of years had been predictable and manageable. One factor in my decision to remain single: I didn't want Allie to think she wasn't the center of my affection—even though I could feel the gradual, inevitable weakening of my gravitational pull on her. Now a sophomore in high school, she would be gone in a couple of years. I didn't like to think about it.

I had indeed found "another line of work." A month shy of six years ago, I became the first life coach Royal Caribbean International—or any cruise line—had hired. The HR woman who interviewed me explained they were looking for someone to "positivize"—her word—the cruising experience for people who fell into conflict or mental disrepair, as well as to give passengers an opportunity to use the time away to re-evaluate their lives. I quickly discovered almost no one took the latter approach. People on a cruise generally want to get *away* from their lives, not go deeper in.

I'd negotiated hard for an exterior cabin—one with a view, tiny though it may be. RCI wanted to put me in a room below the waterline, and while I was desperate to get the job, I held out for a window and they gave it to me. My work life now was different than it had been—which was the whole point of making a change. Except when working with RCI staff, I had only one or two sessions with patients, three at most. Royal Caribbean had been uncertain about whether the coaching gig would work out, so they'd offered me an unusual contract. Unlike most service staff, who had six-month contracts and lived on board 24/7, I shipped out for seven days every other week, which gave me the alternate weeks at home with Allie. The weeks I was at sea, Allie stayed with the family of her lifelong friend, Liz.

When my coffee was ready, I opened my phone and made a FaceTime call. I figured Allie would be up by now and if not, the call would be a good wakeup. The phone rang for what seemed like more than a minute before Allie's face filled the screen, her amber hair framing blue eyes and pencil-thin lips. She was sitting at a desk in her bedroom and, like me, had a cup of coffee in her hand. Her smile was the best thing in my life.

"I slept pretty good," she said, after I asked how she was. "I woke up early and wanted to call but didn't want to wake you."

"You look great," I said. "What are you having for breakfast?"

"The usual. Granola and yogurt with blueberries and extra almonds."

"I thought you wanted to try your hand at making crepes for Liz and her family."

"I do, but I'll save that for Friday. If they turn out okay, I'll make them for you next week."

Gradually, in the weeks and months following that last game of Monopoly, Allie had become my daughter again, if not in quite the same way as before. After that pivotal turning point, her affection for me seemed to hold a measure of reserve. I didn't know how much this was due to her knowledge of my part in the accident in which Claire had died, how much to the natural changes that occur between a father and daughter as she comes more into her own, and how much to Allie being her mother's daughter, holding a part of herself back. Never again since the night of that Monopoly game had Allie mentioned the accident. Of course, she must have thought about it from time to time. I certainly did, even now. Something as mundane as a stoplight turning red could bring the event horrifyingly alive in my mind. One good thing about life at sea: there were no stoplights. My own assessment of the accident had undergone some change. I no longer blamed myself alone. Myself still, but not alone. What had Claire been thinking, raising such an explosive issue in the midst of a difficult traffic negotiation?

Allie continued to have an active concern for climate change and various other vulnerabilities of planet Earth, and about a year after her mother's death she developed a keen interest in astronomy. When she was eleven, I brought her outside to witness a particularly marvelous sunset. "It's not really a sunset, Daddy," she'd said. "It's an earth-turn. You know that, right?"

Recently, she'd spoken of wanting to be an astronaut. This idea I didn't like at all; I couldn't imagine a life where for prolonged periods of time, Allie would be untethered from planet earth. From me. When I asked her why she wanted to be an astronaut, she looked at me like I didn't have a brain. "We're going have to leave Earth someday; I want to have a part in preparing for it."

Allie switched to the outward-looking camera on her phone and maneuvered it until I could see Twosome on a chair next to her. She patted the cat several times, cooing as she stroked its fur, then switched the camera back to herself. "Are you eating breakfast with the crew this morning, or are you going to mingle with the paying customers?"

"The cargo?" I said, smiling.

"The 'cones,' as you like to call them." It was a term taken from the Saturday Night Live "coneheads," who ate massive quantities of food. For obvious reasons, the label was used by cruise ship staff to refer to passengers.

"I'll probably eat with the crew this morning. Save the cones for lunch."

"We'll talk again tonight," she said, rising from the desk. This was our arrangement, two FaceTime conversations a day while I was at sea.

"Okay. I love you."

"Loveyatoo."

I watched her face vanish from my phone, her fingers frozen in a goodbye wave. In moments like this I wondered if I'd made the right decision taking the job with RCI. But there hadn't been any alternatives as good as this one, especially given the pay and benefits I enjoyed.

After a shave and change of clothes, I walked a couple decks down to the crew dining room. As I put food on my plate—scrambled eggs, sausage, toast—I searched for Will, the piano player at the Schooner Bar. I liked Will and had spent the past three evenings listening to him play. It had been a long time since I'd come across someone I wanted to get to know better. Roger and I had lost contact after I quit private practice and I didn't have much in common with most of the RCI crew. Will was a character: an honest man with a winning sense of humor. And a wonderful musician. I didn't see him in the dining room. Probably too early. Either that or he'd decided to eat upstairs. Will liked the attention of the cones.

After breakfast I walked up to my office, an interior room two decks above my living quarters. After catching up on email, I greeted my first appointment of the day, Jack and Bernice Goodwater. Jack was short and slender, Bernice a large woman—it wouldn't be wrong to call her fat. Both looked to be in their early fifties. After we were seated, I asked what I could do for them.

Jack and Bernice looked at one another, then Bernice said, "I want you to tell my husband he's not to dance with other women."

I'd gotten used to the way cruise ship passengers treated my role differently than my psychotherapy patients. To the passengers, "coaching" often meant "instructing," especially when it came to spouses. "So, this happened?" I asked. "He danced with another woman?" I looked first at Bernice and then Jack.

Jack extended his arm into the small room and pointed at his wife. "*She* wouldn't dance with me, so I asked someone else." His expression indicated he clearly thought he had been the injured party.

Early in my career I would have felt annoyed at such a petty conflict. Since then I'd learned how much of life, and especially relational life, is lived in the nitty details. "So, you each suffered a disappointment," I said, meaning to shift their focus from an individual perspective to one that included them both. From the way they looked at one another, with a bit of surprised curiosity softening their features, it seemed neither realized they were having a shared experience.

Before either could recover from this disequilibrium to claim theirs was the most egregious injury, I asked, "Tell me how you came to be on this cruise."

Jack spoke up. "Bernice won it. She was top producer in her real estate agency." He looked at her with pride, and her large face bore a shy smile.

I turned to Bernice. "And you decided to invite this guy along?"

"Well...yes," she said, flustered by the question.

I meant to highlight the fact she'd made a choice, even if it might not have seemed so to her. I looked at one and then the other and asked, "When this cruise is over, what do you want to take away from it?"

Again, Jack spoke first. "A good time."

"Bernice—what about you? What would you like to take away?"

"Good memories."

"A good time. Good memories. Makes sense. Bernice, do you like to dance?"

"Not really."

"Jack, do you feel you *have* to dance, to have a good time?"

"No."

I let silence spool into the room for a moment and then said, "So—what can you do that will give *both* of you a good time? And good memories?"

Jack and Bernice stared blankly at one another. Bernice said, "At home, we like to cook together. Plan meals, go shopping, prepare the food. Jack is all the time searching new recipes for us to try."

I laughed softly, "Not much of an option here, is it? Okay, what else do you do to have fun at home?" The couple looked at each other as though neither knew what to say. "What about before you got married?" I asked. "Anything you liked to do together then?"

A mischievous look came into Jack's eyes. "You mean besides the obvious?"

"I'm sorry," I said. "What's 'the obvious?'" I made myself look genuinely perplexed.

"You know." Jack said.

"No, I'm afraid I don't."

"Sex!" Jack's expression indicated I was an idiot.

I looked at Bernice to see if I could gather any clues about her attitude toward their sex life. She didn't look upset so much as a bit depressed.

I addressed neither of them in particular. "So how have things been going in that department?"

A silence filled the room. Then, "Not so good, Doc," Jack said.

"How come?"

Jack looked to Bernice as though asking her to help him. She wouldn't look at him. He squirmed a bit in his chair. "Bernice don't much care for it anymore."

Bernice's head shot upright and she threw Jack a fierce look. "That's not true and you know it."

"No, Bernice, I don't know it," Jack said with surprising patience. "You told me not to touch you like that again."

Bernice puffed up. "I most certainly did not."

"Remember? Last year? We were in bed and I started touchin' your breasts and you said for me to not do that again."

A little air went out of her. "Your hands were freezing, Jack."

Neither spoke for a length of time that began to feel uncomfortable. I asked Bernice what she was thinking. She turned to Jack. "I thought you quit touching me because I'd gained a lot of weight."

He shook his head. "I've always liked big women. The woman I danced with last night, she was no Twiggy." Bernice gave him a glare. Jack held up his hands. "Truce?" he offered.

Bernice looked at me. "He can be so dense."

"You didn't mean for him to quit touching you altogether," I said.

"No, I did not." Bernice's voice again had a hard edge to it.

I let a moment pass. "So where do we go from here?" I asked.

Jack looked at Bernice. "I think we can take it from here, Doc."

"You good with that?" I asked Bernice. She nodded.

Jack got up from his chair, followed by Bernice. "Thank you," Jack said. "I didn't expect anything would come of us talking to you, but I was wrong." They shook hands and Jack started out the door. As Bernice passed by me, she smiled and mouthed the words, "Thanks, Doc."

The session had gone as well as it could have. Better than most, easier than most. I figured the "truce" I'd helped them achieve would last at least the remainder of the cruise and maybe for some weeks or months after. Eventually, they would likely fall back into another version of the same dynamic: Bernice would come across abrupt and angry without realizing it and Jack would make too much of it and shut down. All I'd done was apply a Band-Aid. These years aboard ship, I'd learned to resist the urge to open a pathway to deeper waters. I was a submariner no more; the limited time available to work with passengers precluded more substantial change.

I missed it, sometimes, the deeper work that brought with it deeper connections. I liked Bernice and Jack, and a part of me wished I could work with them over a longer period of time, where I could help in a more transformational way. The way I used to work. Of course, Jack and Bernice would never know what they'd missed. You don't miss what you can't imagine or haven't experienced. They probably thought I was fabulous. My post-cruise evaluations were generally very high.

As I was making notes of the session, a thought struck me, one of those out-of-the-blue insights that come when you least expect it. I realized that in working as a life coach, I'd consigned myself to repeat, over and over again, the experience I'd had with Ricardo: that of making a good start to lasting change only to cut it short. This thought was more than a bit disconcerting. Was my psyche trying to tell me something? Was I shortchanging myself, punishing myself somehow? If so, for what?

After the morning's work I headed for the Windjammer on Deck 9. With its informal smorgasbord of food options—more varied than the fare in the crew cafeteria—Deck 9 was where most passengers ate. Even those I hadn't worked with often recognized me from posters in their cabins that featured my face and name along with a catchy slogan: "Your Cure for the Cruise Blues." I hated the phrase, but it was what the RCI PR department had churned out.

In the Windjammer, I collected small amounts of many different foods: chicken curry, vegetable lasagna, baked pasta with cheese, sweet and sour chicken, garlic rice. I liked to sample various offerings and then return to get a full serving of what I liked best. Plate full, I headed toward a small, two-seat table next to a window where Will sat by himself.

He waved me in, a big smile on his bearded face. After I sat, Will put his fork down. "Hey, I been meaning to ask, how come I never see you at the crew bar after hours?"

When I first started with the cruise line, I'd often visited the crew bar. But too often, friends I made would get transferred to another ship or their contract would run out. I mentioned this to Will. "I got tired of all the goodbyes."

"The crew and staff talk about you. You're quite the mystery man. 'What's up with the shrink?' they ask me. 'He too good for us?'"

I laughed and took a forkful of sweet and sour chicken. "The shrink, huh?"

"This week some of them have seen you hanging out in the Schooner Bar watching me play. They think I must know a thing or two."

"Do you?" I took another forkful of food.

"One thing I know is, you don't look all that happy. Not for an expert on mental health."

I felt the ship roll with a wave and looked out the window at a sea the color of Allie's eyes. I thought of all the things I'd come to love about working here: the constant movement of the ship, the short but intense relationships with my clients, the time alone in my cabin. Claire's comment, "I need room to breathe," came to mind. Perhaps I was more like her than I'd thought. Then I thought of my insight earlier, how maybe I was shortchanging myself, denying myself a fuller life. "I'm happy enough for now," I said.

A young woman walking away from the food court caught my attention. She looked strikingly like my old patient, Angela, tall and lithe with long black hair. Seeing her sent an electric jolt through me. I thought about leaving the table to see if it might really be her, but then I realized it couldn't be. I turned my attention back to Will, who'd cocked his head to one side, looking at me strangely. "Where'd you go, buddy?" he asked.

"Sorry, got distracted. Anyway, what about you? You happy?"

"I'd be a heck of a lot happier if I could get a job off this god-damned boat."

"Well, why don't you? You're one hell of a piano player."

"Thing is, there's a ton of good piano players out there. It'd be hard to make as much regular money anywhere else." He cut a piece of roast beef and brought it to his mouth, talking around it. "So, what made you quit civilian life and do this?"

"It's a long story. Maybe I'll tell you about it someday."

CHAPTER TWENTY

The next Monday morning I awakened before six, beating the 6:30 alarm I'd set the night before. I liked to rise early the weeks I was home, so I could make breakfast for Allie before she headed to school. This morning I'd planned a blast from the past: french toast. Allie had grown tired of it several years ago, but I thought it was time for a comeback. She walked into the kitchen just as I was placing the bread on the griddle.

"French toast," she said, surprised, holding Twosome in her arms. "We haven't had that in ages." The cat stretched its nose toward the egg-soaked and cinnamon-topped slices of bread.

"Looks like Twosome would like to try a bite," I said. "Remember when I used to make it for you every Sunday?"

"A long time ago." And it was. Our lives were so different now it seemed another lifetime that Claire had been with us.

When the toast was ready, Allie and I sat across from one another at the small kitchen table, Allie working the buttons on her phone. I remembered how she'd done this when she was only nine, sitting in the same chair she sat in now. "What's your day at school look like today?" I asked, wanting her to look at me and not her phone. Just like before.

"The usual," she said, not looking up. "I don't think I've told you about my science teacher." She looked at me. "Have I?"

"No. What about him?"

She attacked the french toast as she spoke. "I really like him. He wanted to be an astronomer, like me, but he had a baby and needed a job, so he never finished his PhD. He'd planned to study black holes which, you know, I'm interested in, too." It struck me as odd she would know so much about her science teacher's life. I asked her about it. She pushed her phone aside. "I have him right before lunch. Sometimes I stay after class and we talk while he eats a sandwich. He agrees with me that our future is not here but among the stars." She looked away, seeming to think about something, and when she looked at me again, a hesitant look came over her. "There's something I need to tell you."

I set my fork down.

"Mr. Roberts—that's my science teacher—he told me about a residency program on the Big Island in Hawaii." Her voice gathered momentum. "It's at the Mauna Kea Observatory, the biggest in the world, with ten or eleven telescopes. Can you imagine *that many?* Mr. Roberts studied there years ago. He still has connections. He nominated me for a place in the program, can you believe it? He thinks I have a good chance of being accepted."

I felt my world shifting out of my control. I understood her excitement—astronomy was her passion—but I couldn't imagine coming home every other week to an empty house, my daughter halfway across an ocean. She wasn't supposed to be gone for two more years. "What about your cat?" I asked, thinking cats surely weren't allowed at the observatory.

"Liz has agreed to keep her while I'm gone."

Allie's already made arrangements for the cat? I wondered how long she'd been thinking about this, planning for it, and why I was hearing about it just now. I tried to sound casual. "When does the program begin?"

"This summer, after the regular school year ends."

"And how long does it last?"

She looked down at her now empty plate, then back up again. "It could last just the summer. Or..." she grimaced in a way that suggested I wouldn't like to hear what she had to say next. "...I could stay for all of my junior year."

I tried to hide my alarm. "Is this something you want to do?"

"Yes," she said, a hint of challenge in her voice.

Again I felt my world, my life, shift before my eyes. Was this the cost of being with Allie only every other week—that I could be so out of touch with what she was thinking? Or had she just been afraid to tell me? "I suppose you need my permission."

"There's a form you need to sign. I might not get in, but I'd like to try. You know, Mom always wanted to go there."

I thought I must have misunderstood her. "Mom wanted to go where?"

"To Hawaii. She said it looked like a paradise. We always said we would go there one day."

Claire had talked about going to Hawaii with Allie? It was inconceivable. But, apparently, true. I felt newly betrayed by Claire that she'd never mentioned it to me. I would've liked to have gone to Hawaii, too. With them.

"Think how well this will set me up for college applications," Allie continued.

She was right. A program like this would give her a real advantage. I ate the last bite of my french toast. It was cold and too sweet. "Mr. Roberts must think a lot of you to recommend you for this program."

"Yeah, he likes me." A smile warmed her face, lit her eyes. "So, can I go?"

How could I possibly answer such a question when I'd just learned about all this? The right answer seemed to be "yes," but… "For the summer or for a year?" I asked.

"At the end of the summer they decide who to keep on."

"If you were invited, would you want to stay?"

"I'd have to see how it is to be there. But…yeah, I think so."

Couldn't you be a little more ambivalent about leaving home, leaving me, for an entire year? "I guess we'll cross that bridge when we come to it."

"I can go for the summer then?"

It was clear she had her heart set on it. "Allie, there's a lot you haven't told me. Do you know where you would stay, how you would live?"

"Mr. Roberts is going to tell me all about that. 'The details,' he calls them. He wants me to come to his house after school one night so we can go over it all."

The idea of Allie going over to a male teacher's house alone was a no-go. I'd never even met the guy, and the extent of Allie's affection for him worried me. "Why don't we invite Mr. Roberts over here? Him and his wife, if he's married. That way you and I can hear the details together."

Allie sat back in her chair. "He doesn't have a wife." Her voice faltered. "She died." A pause. "Like Mom."

"In a car accident?"

"A boating accident."

"What happened?"

"Mr. Roberts' family—he has a daughter who survived—they were on the Intracoastal for the fourth of July and another boat came out of nowhere and plowed into them. Mr. Roberts' wife was still alive when the Coast Guard took her to the hospital, but she didn't make it.

"How old is his daughter?"

"She was nine when it happened." Allie looked at me knowingly. The same age she'd been when Claire died.

"You haven't met his daughter?"

"No, but I'd like to."

"Let's invite her over, too. Give me Mr. Roberts' number and I'll give him a call."

• • •

I studied Frank Roberts across the dining room table. He was short and stocky with close-cut brown hair and intelligent, hazel eyes. Young, not yet thirty. His daughter hadn't come; Frank said she was spending a long weekend with her grandmother. After small talk between Frank and Allie about their pets—Frank had a small, mixed-breed dog named BoBo—Allie told Frank that I wanted to know about living arrangements at the observatory.

"It's beautiful at the summit," Frank said, still speaking to Allie. "You're above the clouds, looking up at a sky filled with more stars than you can imagine." He moved his hands in a high, wide arc. He told Allie that most observations nowadays are conducted remotely, in an office and dormitory complex seven miles down mountain, at a place called Hale Pōhaku. "In the beginning, though, you'll work at the telescopes themselves."

I noted that although Allie had framed the question about living arrangements as my question, Frank was talking only to her. As though I weren't there.

"In addition to the dormitories," Frank continued, "there are common areas—cafeteria, library, laundry room. That sort of thing."

"How cold is it there?" Allie asked, holding her chest with her arms, mimicking being in a freezing cold.

"Not bad. Mid-forties to low sixties. You get used to it. And you can always go down mountain if you want some sun. Hilo, the nearest city, is a little more than an hour away."

It was time I was included in the conversation. "You were there? At the observatory?"

Frank turned to me. "Yes. I was in a PhD program at the University of Hawaii for nine months." He showed me nine fingers.

"How many people live in the dorms?" I asked.

"Seventy-two, seventy-five at the most."

"Any other people Allie's age?"

"Twenty or so high school students come for the summer. A handful get to stay."

Frank's voice had lost its energetic flair. I felt like I was interviewing a reluctant witness. "What about cost?"

"Room and board are included in the program. Any spending money outside of that is up to you and Allie."

"So, what's the downside? There's got to be one."

Frank shrugged. "What you'd expect, I guess. Social life is limited. Most of the time, Allie will be stuck at the dormitory complex. It's a pretty narrow world geographically but exciting intellectually." Frank turned back to Allie, his voice picking up tempo. "You'll get to interact with people from all over the world."

Her voice was soft. "It sounds good, Daddy."

"Daddy." I wondered if her use of the word was strategic. "We can talk about it," I told her.

After Frank left, Allie and I sat at opposite ends of the sofa with Twosome in between. Allie was a beautiful girl, with fine, sharply drawn features, long, sand-colored hair and closely spaced, marble-blue eyes. She seemed too young to go off for a year on her own. But I remembered how I felt when I was just one year older, sixteen. I'd left home for good then, having graduated from an experimental program that condensed four years of High School into three. I hadn't gone as far away as she'd be going, but I'd felt old enough to be on my own. She probably felt that way, too.

I put my hand on Twosome's back and the cat gave a grunt of disapproval before moving just out of reach. "So. You want to try this?" I asked Allie.

"Yes, I do."

"You realize everything you'll be giving up? The high school scene. Your friends. Dating."

She laughed. "You wouldn't let me date."

"Well—I don't mean *dating* dating. More hanging out with girls and guys both."

She picked up her phone and studied something on it. "There'll be plenty of time for that when I come back for my senior year."

"You're talking as though you plan to stay the whole year."

She looked up from her phone. "I want to."

I didn't mention something else she'd be giving up: time with me. I had little idea what that meant to her, if anything. Did she even think about it? I started to ask if she would miss me but that seemed too maudlin, and I wasn't sure I wanted to know anyway. I asked about the cat instead. "What about Twosome? Won't you miss her?"

"Miss her like crazy," she said, rubbing her hands along Twosome's body. The cat rolled over on her back and lifted her head to Allie, who put down her phone so she could stroke Twosome's tummy. A mammoth purr ensued.

That she was so eager to spend a year apart when we had so little time left before she went off to college worried me. I thought we'd gotten a good bit closer these past few years.

Had I been wrong?

CHAPTER TWENTY-ONE

On the *Allure of the Seas,* I was at a late Sunday lunch with Will when, again, I thought I saw a woman that looked like Angela leave the food court. This time I excused myself and went to get a better look. The woman had been wearing blue shorts and a white top; I quickly spotted her walking toward the stern of the ship. I watched, transfixed, as Angela Morales appeared and disappeared among the throng of passengers. It was as though she were a figure in a dream. Seeing her, I felt both attracted and repelled.

I had a chilling thought: Was Ricardo on board as well? Surely by this time she'd gotten free of the man. He had, after all, let her go. I wondered if I could arrange to "accidentally" run into Angela, find out what had become of her life. Then I remembered: My face, my name, was ubiquitous on the ship. She had to know I was on board. Was it mere coincidence she was here, then, or had she discovered I worked this cruise ship and booked her cruise in order to reconnect? That seemed unlikely. If she wanted to complete a course of psychotherapy with me, one week would do little to accomplish that goal. And our last contact had been anything but friendly.

My appetite gone, I returned to the table and told Will I wasn't feeling well. Not a lie. I returned to my living quarters to think things through. I almost never had an appointment on Sunday, the first day of the cruise and a partial one at that. But today I had one, in a little more than an hour. The woman who'd signed up hadn't given her full name, only her initials. I opened my electronic appointment book and saw "AM" written there. It was as though six years dropped away as quickly as a curtain slipped from its rod. A part of me was curious to see Angela again, to find out what her life was like now. But another part of me knew the ship was still docked. It wasn't too late to head home.

• • •

Angela sat across from me in my office, her eyes searching mine with almost physical force. Even after all these years, it was as though I held something essential to her being. And just as before, I was drawn in. But I also felt a shadow of the old dread. So much had gone wrong the last time we'd worked together.

"Dr. Paul, you don't seem surprised to see me."

"I saw you at lunch today. I was plenty surprised then." My eyes tracked hers as she glanced around the room. It contained a desk and three chairs, none of which were particularly comfortable. No windows. Unlike my old office in Miami Shores, there were few personal belongings, only a recent picture of Allie. Angela's gaze settled on me again. "What brings you here?" I asked, the age-old first question.

"We have unfinished business, Dr. Paul." She said this matter-of-factly, but I could feel the weight of our aborted work together, both how promising it had been in the beginning and how painful its ending. "I am ready to leave Ricardo," she said. "For good, this time."

The sense of *déjà vu* was dizzying. "You mean…you never left?" The gentle, nearly imperceptible bumping of the ship through the water, normally a comfort to me, now made me nearly nauseous.

She sat unmoving, her eyes on mine for long moments. I couldn't tell whether she was angry, or simply sorry about how things had ended between us. "After you quit working with me," she finally said, weariness coloring her voice, "I went back to him."

I could imagine what that had meant: All hope for a life of her own, gone. "But why?" I asked.

"Ricardo was relentless. He talked about how important I was to him, how he wanted to hurt me but couldn't, how he'd never felt that way about anyone else." Angela closed her eyes for a moment, then opened them again. "I didn't have you to lean on, or anyone for that matter, so I gave in. And Ricardo did seem different. I could tell I truly mattered to him." She gave me a meaningful look. "Something happened in your work with him, Dr. Paul. Something big."

I was aware of feeling a depth of care for Angela I didn't have for my coaching clients. I took a breath and refocused. "What was it like, going back to Ricardo?"

"It was safe." I angled my head, not comprehending what she'd meant. She smiled. "You know, like the safety of a prison cell." When Angela spoke again, there was melancholy in her voice. "Even though I could tell I was super important to Ricardo, it was like he still wanted to own me. He talked me into quitting my job at the bank and my courses at the college. He said these things were not necessary now." She lifted her hand to brush hair out of her eyes and I felt a wrenching in my gut. The tip of the index finger on her right hand was missing.

"What happened to your finger?" My words bore the alarm I felt. She looked at the foreshortened digit. "*Jesus,*" I said. I thought I knew what must have happened. "You said he didn't hurt you."

"Well, there was that one time."

I asked with my eyes for her to tell me what had happened.

"I bit off the tip of his tongue, so he cut off the tip of my finger. He said it was the only way he could forgive me. He thought about cutting off the tip of *my* tongue, but he said it had 'other uses.' I don't know why I let him do it." Again, I heard the defeat in her voice, a giving up on herself. I couldn't help but wonder how Ricardo had accomplished the amputation, but to ask would be macabre. Angela rubbed her thumb across the amputated finger.

I'd lost track of what we'd been talking about, so I tried a reset. "How did you find out I was working for the cruise line?"

"I read it in a travel magazine. There was an article on a new service cruise lines were starting to offer. I looked into it and found out you worked for RCI, so I booked the next cruise. That was week before last. But I chickened out on talking to you. I spent most of the time holed up in my room."

So it had been her the last time. A sense of unreality set in, my old life catching up with me. "Tell me again why you're here?" I asked.

"I am ready now to leave Ricardo, but not strong enough to do it on my own."

"I don't understand. What has changed? If I help you leave Ricardo, won't I be in danger again?" I remembered the deal Ricardo and I had made: that if we worked together, Ricardo would give Angela her freedom. But had he been serious? And if so, was he still?

Angela waved her hand in dismissal. "You don't need to worry about Ricardo. To him, you are like a god."

I looked at her in disbelief.

"When we first got back together, he talked about you all the time, how he didn't expect you could help him, but you did."

Could this be true? My work with Ricardo, which had driven me straight out of the profession, had been a success? I doubted it; we hadn't worked together that long. Besides, Ricardo *had* cut off the tip of Angela's finger. I had to tell Angela I couldn't work with her. I no longer even had a license to practice. "Angela, I don't do therapy anymore," I told her.

She slowly shook her head. "It doesn't matter to me what you call it. Therapy. Coaching. Whatever."

I could have explained how they aren't the same, but I didn't think it would matter. Surely, though, she could see that the logistics of working together were impossible. "Angela, my only office is on this ship. We could work together only every other week, and you'd have to buy a cruise ticket every time."

She gave a slight smile. "You forget, Dr. Paul, I have access to considerable wealth. The cruise ticket is nothing to me. And because of Ricardo's contacts, I get a discount. Every other week is fine. But when I'm here, we work every day, right?"

An image came to mind of an insect being gathered into a spider's web. Yet I was intrigued. Something unfinished in my life might be made whole.

"Dr. Paul. Every day, right?"

"I think twice a week is about all we could make good use of."

Angela held up three fingers. "How about three: Sunday, Wednesday, Friday."

"How can I be sure that working with you will not endanger me?"

Angela leaned forward. "Ricardo has changed. Even though he did cut off the tip of my finger, I'm not sure he would have done it if I hadn't stupidly agreed to it. He used to have a violent edge to him nearly all the time, something almost tangible. You could feel it. He doesn't have that anymore."

I didn't doubt Angela believed what she was saying was true. And who would know Ricardo better? "Okay," I said, "three times a week. But let's make it Monday, Wednesday and Friday. And only if it remains productive." Angela gave a quick nod of her head. I noticed again her amputated finger, its missing tip. I'd read somewhere that there are finger prosthetics, artificial fingertips. "Your finger, couldn't you have an artificial tip made for it?"

She studied the finger. "Yes, I asked about that but Ricardo wouldn't pay for it. He said it would 'betray the point.'"

"I don't get it."

"I think what Ricardo meant was, he couldn't get an artificial tongue, so it wouldn't be fair for me to get an artificial finger."

I studied Angela. Maybe I should tell her the most I could offer was some coaching. But if I were to do that, she would turn it into therapy. Probably, I would, too. Therapy was what she needed. And it was what a part of *me* needed, too, to pick up the work I'd abandoned. I thought about how shallow my work life had become and suddenly everything I'd loved about living and working aboard ship felt like a confinement. *The safety of a prison cell.*

"You mentioned you aren't strong enough to leave Ricardo," I said. "Not strong enough on your own. Tell me more about that."

Even though I hadn't practiced real therapy in six years, I felt myself slipping back into the role. Not just a role, an identity.

"When I left Ricardo before," she said, "I couldn't stay away. I was too…lonely. It was…what's the word? Not breathable."

I imagined the word she wanted was "suffocating" but didn't correct her. She'd described it perfectly. "Can you recall that feeling now?" I asked. "The unbreathable loneliness?"

Something within her seemed to shrink. "Yes."

"Who are you lonely for?"

There was a hint of surprise on her face and she looked inward. "I felt this way also when I was on the airplane coming into this country."

"You were lonely on the airplane?"

A hollow look came into Angela's pale eyes and she spoke as if in a dream. "Yes."

"Who were you lonely for?"

"My grandmother."

"Pietra."

Angela's eyes became liquid and she drew a sharp intake of breath. "You remember."

I was surprised, too, that I'd remembered her grandmother's name. A silence lingered, and it occurred to me that Angela seemed nearly without skin, that she could be devoured by feeling, whether it be fear or desire. She could be taken over. Had been taken over. By Ricardo, by her mother's boyfriend. By her father. She was asking me to take her over now, so I could return her to herself. It was my job, my calling. But I knew that if we were to work together again, we had to talk about how the earlier work had ended. "Angela," I said, "you sought me out. You booked this cruise and made an appointment with me."

"Yes."

"How did you know I would talk to you? The last time we were together, I threw you out of my office." I thought this was harsher than she would have put it, but I didn't want to pretend it had been anything but that.

I could see her swallow. "Yes," she said, "that did happen."

"So…what is it like to sit across from me now?"

She looked down, rubbed her lost fingertip. "It was difficult to come. It's why I chickened out before. I was afraid you might, as you say, throw me out again."

I waited for her to say more but instead she looked at me coolly, as if from a distance. I decided to make a path forward by tracking closely what she'd last said. I spoke carefully, as though my words might wound her. "It was difficult. You thought I might throw you out again."

Light came into her eyes. "I was desperate. Too much of my life had been already lost. And I know it is therapy that I need to… to find a way forward."

I spoke softly. "You could work with someone else."

"Ricardo respects you. Some stranger…no. Besides, I did try another therapist a few years ago. She was just, how do you put it, going through motions. She didn't really care."

"I don't know if I can help you or not," I said, "but I'm willing to try." At this, Angela visibly relaxed. After a moment, I added, "I think it took much courage for you to seek me out again. I admire you for that." There was no visible response on her face or in her eyes. I didn't have a clue what she was experiencing. "What is it like for you to hear me say this?" I asked. "That I admire your courage?"

She smiled, and there was in her eyes a hint of laughter. "It makes me think you do not know me as well as I thought."

"So, it is hard for you to trust I really mean it?" She nodded. "How did Pietra do it? How did she become someone whose word you trusted?"

Angela angled her head to one side. "I'm not sure."

"What might it have been?"

She thought for a moment. "I think it was because she didn't want anything from me. Or need anything."

"And with me?" Paul asked.

"I pay you a fee."

I gave a small laugh. "Actually, you won't, not this time. The cruise line pays my salary. But even if you were still paying a fee, do you think my opinions, my feelings, could be bought?"

She looked at me thoughtfully. "Ricardo bought you."

"What do you mean?"

"You know, when you quit working with me. Ricardo made you an offer you couldn't refuse. He could pay you…anything."

Apparently, she had misconstrued my meaning when I'd told her Ricardo had made an offer I couldn't refuse. He must not have told her about his "fee." I leaned forward and held her eyes with mine. "Ricardo didn't buy me. He threatened to break my legs if I didn't work with him." Angela looked at first surprised, then guilty, as though *she'd* been the one to do me harm. "You're not responsible for his actions," I said. I glanced at the clock on the wall above her.

Angela saw me do this and she checked the one on the table between us. "It is almost time," she said, reaching for her purse. "It feels strange, not to pay you a fee. Can I pay something anyway?"

Allie's college was on the horizon; I could use the extra cash. And occasionally, satisfied customers would designate a tip for me at the end of the cruise. But I didn't mention this to Angela. "I'm paid by the cruise line. Let's leave it at that." She put her purse down, folded her hands in her lap. "There are still five minutes left," I said. "Tell me what you'd like to accomplish in our work together. What will it look like if we are successful?"

Angela thought for a moment. "I want to make a life of my own—and I want to be strong enough to resist Ricardo when he tries to get me to come back."

"How will you know you're strong enough? What will tell you that?"

"Won't I just feel it?"

"My guess is, when you're strong enough to resist Ricardo, your behavior with him will already have changed in other ways."

She nodded her head.

It was time to ask the hard question, the necessary question. "Have you told Ricardo you came here so you could work with me again?"

She looked away. "No." When she looked at me again, there was worry in her eyes. "It will cause…problems."

"Angela, I thought you said Ricardo wouldn't try to harm me."

She shook her head. "No, nothing like that. He'll be angry with me, not you."

I waited a beat. "What is it like when he's angry with you?"

"I feel…cornered."

"Can you say more?"

"The anxiety, it is very bad."

"So maybe you need someone in the corner with you?"

She smiled shyly, with a hint of pleasure in her turquoise eyes, so pale they seemed unnatural. "Yes. I would like you in the corner with me."

I was smiling, too. "Let's meet again in three days. Wednesday."

After Angela left, I sat in the small office reflecting on what had happened. We'd made a good beginning. And for forty-five minutes, I'd used parts of my skill set and aspects of myself I hadn't exercised in many years. It occurred to me that this work would not only be about helping Angela. It would be about helping me as well.

CHAPTER TWENTY-TWO

Sunday evening, home from the cruise, Angela knew she had to tell Ricardo what she'd done. She lay in bed reading the news on her phone; Ricardo sat in a chair by the bedside table. There was nothing to do but, how do you say it? *Eat the bullet.*

"Ricardo," she said, putting her phone down. "There's something I need to tell you."

"Mmmm?" he muttered, not looking up from a legal document.

"You know the cruise I went on last week?"

"Mhmmm."

"It wasn't just a cruise."

When he muttered a third time, she said, "Ricardo. Look at me."

He looked at her with annoyance. "I already told you I do not mind that you went on the cruise. But you should have told me ahead of time."

"It wasn't just a cruise," she repeated. He set the document down on the bedside table and looked at her in a way that let her know he was finally listening. "I signed up for that cruise because I knew Dr. Mason would be on it."

Surprise registered on Ricardo's face. "How could you know such a thing?"

"He works there now. He's what they call a "life coach." Ricardo looked confused. She was sure he had no idea what a "life coach" was, or even that such a thing existed.

"Why did you want to see him?" he asked, and then understanding came into his eyes. He spoke quickly. "You are seeing him for therapy again, no?"

She sat up in the bed, leaned against the headboard. She remembered what Dr. Paul had said about being in her corner. Maybe, with his help, she could stand up to Ricardo. "Yes," she said. Ricardo took a bottle of Scotch from the table and poured it into a glass. When he looked up, his eyes were darker than before. She didn't like that he'd made himself a drink. The conversation would be difficult enough with him sober. "I'm not *happy*, Ricardo. Can't you tell?"

He took a hefty portion of the drink, then looked at the glass while he swirled the ice around. "I can't tell a fucking thing with you." He looked at her now. "If you want me to know what's in your head, you have to 'use your words.'" He made sarcastic air quotes around the phrase, 'use your words,' a phrase he'd learned from her. "C'mon, Angie, what is it?" He picked up the drink and took another swallow.

"It's not you, *personally*," she said.

"What the fuck does that mean?" When she didn't answer, he stood and began to pace about the room. "Give me the whole story, not just the headline."

She sighed. "I know you, Ricardo. You don't really want the whole story."

He stopped pacing and looked at her. "I do."

"And you'll listen? You won't interrupt?" He grunted and took in more of the Scotch, squeezing his lips tight together as though what he'd consumed had been surprisingly bitter. "I'm not happy," she continued, "because I don't have a life. You won't divorce your wife, even though you hardly ever see her. You won't pay for me to finish my education. And you won't let me work. I'm just an accessory to *your* life, which...you never let me in on."

"You know I cannot talk about my work. It is confidential."

"I'm sure other attorneys find a way to communicate *something* about what they've done during the day."

"Some things I do, they go beyond the law. You know this. I keep these things from you to protect you."

This was going nowhere. All Ricardo knew how to do was argue; it was his profession. She wanted to go outside, sit by the pool, but if she did, he'd just follow her there. She leaned back in the bed and closed her eyes. He sat on the bed beside her, causing her to be a little off-balance. She righted herself with her hand. "Tell me about this 'therapy,'" he said, halfway calm again.

She didn't open her eyes. "I can't talk to you about it, Ricardo. It's *confidential*."

He stood and slammed his drink down on the bedside table, spilling Scotch and ice. "Goddammit, don't play the games with me. Dr. Mason closed up shop years ago."

She opened her eyes and looked at the ceiling. There was a baby lizard there, a tiny thing with ridiculously small feet. She wondered how it had gotten inside. "Like I said, he works on a cruise ship now. I plan to see him again next week."

Ricardo had been mopping up the spilled drink with Kleenex. Now he whirled around and faced her. "*What?*"

"I've already booked the cruise." The lizard hadn't moved at all.

"You are going on a cruise just to have therapy with Dr. Mason?"

"Yes, Rickie."

"You talk like that, you *need* therapy. And don't call me Rickie."

"Whatever."

"Angie, look at me."

She did.

"Are you planning to leave again?"

She was surprised to see he was not so much angry as afraid. Still, she wasn't prepared to tell him she was leaving. When she was ready to do so, she'd simply leave and tell him later.

"Answer me," Ricardo said.

"I don't know what I'm going to do. It's why I'm in therapy."

"Find someone else," Ricardo said. "Dr. Mason is my therapist." He picked up the glass, studied the remaining Scotch. "I may need him again."

Angela didn't hide her anger. "You stole him from me, Ricardo." She searched the ceiling but couldn't find the lizard anywhere. She was amused by the thought that the lizard had been Dr. Paul in disguise, listening in. It was a comfort to think so. And not so wrong, because she would tell Dr. Paul about this conversation next time she saw him. She looked down again and saw Ricardo walk out of the bedroom, then heard him slam the door.

Hard.

CHAPTER TWENTY-THREE

"Breakfast is on the table," I called to Allie, who was in her room getting ready for school. I'd decided to start a new tradition; the first morning home after a week at sea, I'd make blueberry pancakes. If I had just six months with Allie before she left for Hawaii, I wanted to make the most of it. I'd even thought about quitting my job with the cruise line, but—what else would I do? As I'd told Angela, I no longer had a license to practice therapy. Of course, I could reactivate my license. I'd have to log quite a few hours of continuing education, but these days the courses could be taken online. I decided to look into it.

Allie arrived at the breakfast table talking excitedly on her phone. To whomever she was speaking, she said, "That sounds so great. I'd love to come." Still standing, I served myself some pancakes from the pile on the table and asked who she'd been talking to. "Mr. Roberts. He invited me over next week to look at pictures of the dormitory complex at Hale Pōhaku."

"Mr. Roberts invited you over where?"

"To his house. We'll catch dinner together and look at the pictures."

I wasn't about to let my teenage daughter go to her widowed teacher's house to "look at pictures." I made myself sit down before I said anything, so I wouldn't be towering over her. "Allie, how well do you know Mr. Roberts?"

"Huh?"

"Do you think it's appropriate for you to go over to a teacher's house to have dinner?"

"God, *Paul.* He's just being nice. Besides, his daughter will be there."

I didn't like the "Paul." She'd started using it again a while back whenever she was annoyed with me. "How do you know his daughter will be there? Did he say so?"

She looked up from her plate and cocked her head to one side, her words laced with sarcasm. "Do you want me to call Mr. Roberts back and say, 'My daddy wants to know if your daughter will be there?'"

"I'm only looking out for your best interests," I said, managing my anger at her dismissive attitude.

"And treating me like a twelve-year-old."

I put my fork down, looked at her. "You don't think it's possible Mr. Roberts is interested in you?"

She made a disgusted face. "*Eeww.* You're weird." She brought a forkful of pancake to her mouth and with her free hand picked up her phone and began texting.

I wondered if it was Frank she was texting and if they were writing back and forth about what a weirdo I was. I opened the newspaper, found the sports section and checked the scores from the golf tournament last weekend. As I read and she continued to play with her phone, I wondered if the fact I'd brought the paper to the table signaled to Allie my lack of interest in having a conversation, inadvertently inviting her to focus on her phone, and I decided to make an effort to engage her. I could tell she was enjoying the pancakes, eating them with relish. I told her there were more warming in the oven and asked if she wanted one.

"Sure," she said, looking up from her phone.

I brought her two more pancakes, and after she'd carefully spread butter to the edges of the pancakes and poured a thin line of syrup on top of the butter, I said I had a proposition. "Why don't I go with you to Mr. Roberts' house? I want to see what it's like, this place you're going to."

She put the bottle of syrup down and shrugged her assent.

"Which means," I reminded her, "you'll have to change the date from next week to the week after. I'll be at sea next week. Unless Mr. Roberts can do it this week."

Allie looked at me with a pained expression. "Do you have to go back to that stupid boat? Can't you call in sick or something?"

"Mr. Roberts can't do it this week?"

"He's taken the week off to go to the National Geographic Explorers Week in Washington. He goes every year."

"It'll have to be week after next then."

"Daddy, do you have to go with me? I could tell you about it after."

Probably, she'd used the "Daddy" to butter me up. Still, it felt good. "I don't *have* to go," I said. "But I'd like to. I want to be a part of this Hawaii adventure."

Allie wrinkled her nose. "You do?"

"Of course."

"You're not coming with me to Mr. Roberts' house just to check on me? You know—with the child-molesting science teacher?"

"Well, there is that. But seriously, I do want to be a part of this Hawaii thing. As much as you'll let me." She looked at me without speaking but her expression was one of suspicion, as though I must be hiding my true intentions.

After I dropped her off at school, it came to me that she'd referred to the cruise ship as *that stupid boat.* In the beginning of my career as a life coach, she'd sometimes complained about my leaving for the week, but she would just as often express excitement about spending the week with Liz and her family. I thought the arrangement worked well for both of us. Was it possible she resented the cruise ship the way I sometimes resented her phone?

That night Allie and I sat on opposite ends of the couch, Allie texting on her phone while I read a novel. Her phone rang, and I could tell from her side of the conversation she was speaking with Liz. They talked for some minutes about Liz's interest in one of the guys at school. Typically, I would retreat to my room at this point or to the screened porch to continue reading. This time I decided to stay. I studied her as she talked. She was very expressive, full of advice for Liz. Good advice. After she ended the conversation, she glanced over at me. "That was good advice you gave Liz," I said. "Take it slow with the guy, get to know him better before letting her heart or hormones take over." I smiled with affection. "How'd you get so smart?"

Allie, returning my smile, blushed. "In a situation like that I ask myself, 'What would Mom say?'"

I had no idea she'd been having dialogues with her dead mother. "You think often of Claire?"

"All the time. I think about what she would want me to do or say in, you know, different situations."

How could I have not known this? "How come I never knew that?" I asked.

Allie looked down at her hands, then up again. "I didn't want to make you uncomfortable."

"Why would I be uncomfortable?"

"You don't like to talk about Mom."

She was both right and not right. I didn't like to talk about how Claire died; in fact, I was afraid it might come up even now and spoil the moment between us. But I didn't mind talking about Claire *per se*. I wished we talked about her more. I wondered how many other false assumptions Allie and I held about one another—incomplete truths that hid deeper complexities? "Sometimes I'm uncomfortable," I said. "You're right about that. But generally, I like to talk about your mother. I especially like to hear what you think about her."

Allie's phone rang again and this time it was a boy she liked. She left the couch and headed to her room to have the conversation, but before she closed her bedroom door, she turned and casually blew me a kiss. I couldn't recall her ever having done that before. This unexpected bloom of intimacy we'd just experienced—it wouldn't have happened if I'd followed my usual routine, if I hadn't *stayed.* I made a decision then to spend more time with Allie before she left for a year. Not just more time. A different kind of time.

CHAPTER TWENTY-FOUR

On the *Allure,* Angela Morales was casually dressed in red shorts and an oversized white T-shirt with the word "Bahamas" in playful blue lettering. She looked worried, her brow furrowed. Since the beginning of the session, she'd avoided eye contact except for quick, darting glances. I wondered what was up.

"After I leave Ricardo," she asked, "will you still work with me?" Her eyes narrowed. "No matter what?"

There must be something she wasn't saying. "Where does this question come from?" I asked.

"I want to be sure, that's all." A pleading look came into her eyes.

I couldn't promise "no matter what" because things might happen that were out of my control. I told her this and then said, "But it is my intention to work with you after you leave Ricardo. To my way of thinking, that's the whole point." I asked if she'd spoken to Ricardo about being back in therapy with me.

She hesitated. "I did. But I wish I hadn't."

"What happened?"

"He got mad."

Just as she'd predicted. "And what was that like for you?"

She smiled shyly. "I thought about what you said about being in my corner. I actually imagined you were there, in the room with me, and it helped. But Ricardo said I should find someone else to work with. He said you were *his* therapist."

I hadn't considered the possibility Ricardo might want to work with me again. Of course, he may have said that just to get Angela to bow out.

"He asked if I was leaving him."

"And what did you tell him?"

"I said I didn't know, that's why I'm in in therapy."

"But you do know…so why didn't you say so?"

"Because then I'd have to get serious about leaving."

"Okay, let's talk about that. What would it take for you to get serious about it?"

With one hand she brushed charcoal hair from her face. "Well, it helps to know you'll be here for me after I leave." A stretch of silence played out before she spoke again, and when she did there was hesitation in her voice. "Sometimes, I talk to you in my head." Her brow furrowed. "Is that weird?"

I remembered what Allie had told me about talking to her mother. "It's natural to talk to people in your head," I said. "Especially if they're important to you."

Angela's face brightened. "Just this morning, I talked to you in the shower."

The thought of Angela in the shower stirred in me more than professional feelings, but she seemed innocent of how I might have taken what she'd said. I asked what she talked to me about.

"How grateful I am you agreed to see me again. If it's true I can keep seeing you after I leave Ricardo, I think I'll be able to do it."

I leaned back in my chair. "What will be hardest, you think, about leaving him?"

"The loneliness. And the uncertainty I feel about who I am apart from him." She paused a tick before adding, "We'll figure that out together, right?" She said this quickly, as though she was afraid I might slip away while she wasn't looking. At first, I thought of this as an irrational fear or an inability to trust. Then I remembered. I *had* slipped away from her once before.

"Yes, we'll figure that out together," I said. Then I asked if she could say more about her concern about who she would be apart from Ricardo.

She lowered her eyes and thought for some moments. For me, there was something sacred about this, about Angela searching for the personal, unique truth within her while I gave her the space and safety to do so. She looked up at me. "I think it has to do with how Ricardo has always taken care of me. Without him to depend on, will I be able to take care of myself?"

"What might keep you from doing so?"

Another silence ensued as she looked inward again. Finally, she offered one word. She offered it as a question. "Fear?"

"Fear of…?"

She closed her eyes and covered her face with her hands. When she took her hands away, she said, "I don't know. Maybe—will I have the strength to do what needs to be done? To meet the challenges. To overcome the loneliness."

I leaned forward. "Remember when you told your mother's boyfriend you would cut off his penis if he didn't leave you alone?"

She smiled. "Yes."

"Was that a strong thing to do?"

Her smile broadened. "Yes."

"So where did that strength come from?"

A sheepish look came into her eyes. "Me."

We spent the rest of the session exploring these issues of her strength, her ability to depend upon me for support, and how little genuine support she'd experienced throughout her life, apart from Pietra. When the session was over, I felt good about it. More than good. Angela seemed close to being ready to make a move and stick with it. And I felt something in me was being restored as well. I was working at a greater depth and continuity than I had in many years.

After the session I headed for the Schooner Bar, where Will was just finishing a set. "Taking a break?" I asked him.

"I am indeed. Care to join me?"

"It's why I came."

We went below decks to the crew bar, away from the attention both of us might attract upstairs. Sometimes I felt claustrophobic below the waterline, but this time it didn't bother me. After both of us ordered drinks, Will asked me how my week away had been.

"I'm a little worried about my daughter." I told him about Allie's plans to spend her junior year in Hawaii.

"She's just in high school and already wants to study halfway across the world? Pretty gutsy."

I was about to tell him our plan to have dinner with Allie's science teacher, to learn more about where in Hawaii she would be staying, when Will drew my attention to a woman walking our way. She looked to be in her early forties. My age. Will caught her eye. "Lynn, there's someone I want you to meet." The woman walked over to our table and Will introduced her. "I feel like we're in Alcoholics

Anonymous," he said, laughing. "I don't know either of your last names."

Lynn eyed me closely, as though studying a strange creature. "So you're the shrink on board." And then, in an affected Southern dialect, "Ah do believe there's a pictcha of you in mah cabin." To Will, she said, "Smith. My last name's Smith."

Will laughed again. "Like hell it is."

"No, really," Lynn said. "I know it's hackneyed, but...Smith it is."

Will made an elaborate gesture of welcome. "Well, won't you join us, Ms. Smith?" She did and the three of us ordered drinks. I asked Lynn what she did on board.

She slanted her head and several strands of dirty-blonde hair fell across her cheek. "I'm a cocktail waitress in the Schooner Bar. I serve while Will plays." She turned and raised her glass to Will. To me, she winked and said, "He brings in the girls, I get the boys."

I asked why I'd never seen her there.

"I just started last week so I'm, like, new here." I asked what had led her to work on a cruise ship. "A bad breakup." She downed some of her drink, lime green with a cherry on top. "How about you?"

I started to say I'd gotten tired of traditional therapy, which was the answer I usually gave, but I felt an unexpected connection with Lynn and decided to tell the truth. "I got into a situation I didn't know any other way out of."

She set her drink down, leaned in. "That is absolutely intriguing. What sort of situation was it?"

"I had a psychotherapy practice and there was a patient I didn't want to work with. However, he insisted." Without using names, I told Lynn and Will about Ricardo's "fee," and about how I'd quit my practice in part because I was afraid he might show up again.

Will looked skeptical. "You really think he would've had your legs broken?"

Lynn spoke before I could. "Of course Paul thought the man would have his legs broken. Otherwise, he wouldn't have cast his lot with the likes of us." She looked at me and tilted her head again, a mischievous look in her eyes. "Am I right?"

I was drawn to Lynn, an attraction I hadn't felt in—well, since Claire died. Lynn's face was rather plain; if I saw a photograph of her, I wouldn't look twice. But her face *in motion* was something else. It held an animated, playful loveliness. I turned to Will. "She's right. I do think he would have done it. That case drove me right out of the profession."

"Out of the fire and into the frying pan?" Lynn asked, still with that mischievous, flirty look.

"I suppose so," I said. The color of Lynn's eyes was hard to pin down. Not brown, not blue. Something in between.

"But do you miss it? The fire?" She was serious now, in a way that made me think she knew a thing or two about fire, its allure as well as its danger.

"I do, actually. I haven't let myself know that until recently."

"What was it that opened your eyes?" Lynn widened her eyes a bit to illustrate her question.

"A woman I've started working with here on the ship. Don't tell anyone, but I'm actually doing therapy with her, not just coaching." I set my glass down and leaned back in my chair. "In fact, she's the girlfriend of the man I was telling you about earlier."

Will mimed an exaggerated double-take. "Man, talk about going straight back into the fire!"

I had to admit, now I was talking about it, working with Angela did seem a bit risky. "My patient assures me I'm not in any danger this time."

"And you *believe* her?" Lynn placed her hand on the upper part of my arm and gave it a squeeze. "Dr. Paul, what sort of experience do you have with women who *want* something from you?" A playful half-smile lingered on her face. It felt good, her touch. "Just a warning," she said and lifted her hand from my arm so she could waggle her forefinger back and forth again in front of my face.

"What about you?" I asked. "What about a breakup sent you scurrying into the sea?"

A frown wrinkled her forehead. "I broke up with Mark because I couldn't trust him." She squinted her eyes. "Or he broke up with me, I'm not sure which. I kept thinking he was cheating on me. He denied it, but there were way too many things that didn't add up. He'd come home and I'd find a blond hair on the collar of his shirt. Yeah, I actually went through his dirty clothes, that's how bad it got. He told me the hair probably came from his friend, Rob, whose hair *is* that color. But I didn't think he would be getting close enough to Rob for Rob's hair to be on his clothing. The clincher came when he returned from a night out with 'the guys'"—here she made elaborate quotation marks—"sporting a red mark on his neck." She pointed to a place on my neck and gave her finger a playful push, hard enough to cause me to wince. "I asked him about it and he said I was crazy. I looked again and couldn't be sure what it was, but it was *something*, not nothing. The next morning, he said, 'Look, if you don't trust me you should leave.' And so I did."

"But why a cruise ship?"

Lynn brought her greenish drink to her mouth and looked at me from above the rim of the glass. "I have a history of jumping into another relationship too fast after one ends badly. Or ends at all. Well, of course, they all end badly, don't they?" She pulled free a strand of hair that had gotten stuck to her face and took a drink from the glass. "I figured out here on the open sea, I'll be safe. I don't have superficial relationships or one-nighters, and out here that's all there are."

For someone who wasn't interested in getting together, Lynn was being awfully flirtatious, I thought. Was I reading into the situation something that wasn't there? Projecting my own interest onto her?

Will spoke up. "Look, I've got some things to take care of before my next set. I'll leave you two alone."

We watched him walk away. Lynn leaned in to me and in a conspiratorial voice asked, "Do you think he's trying to set us up?"

I swirled the ice in my glass. "I was wondering the same thing. In fact, I was wondering if you were in on it."

Lynn, laughing, practically choked on her drink, liquid dribbling between her lips. "Well, you just upped the ante on our little chat."

"Don't take it the wrong way. I'm pretty careful when it comes to…seeing people." *Careful as in I never go there at all.* "Look, I like you. Maybe I should have just said that."

Lynn leaned forward and set her drink on the table. "So, Paul, here's my dilemma, and I'll be frank about it. Why not, since we just met?" The next part she said under her breath, more to herself than to me. "I can't figure out whether I like you, or I like that you like me so much."

Laughing, I said, "You must think I like you a *lot.*"

She leaned back, lifted her drink to her lips and said, "As a matter of fact, I do." After finishing her drink in one swift swallow, she smiled, slid her chair back and stood. "My shift starts in five minutes." She extended her hand and offered a thoroughly businesslike handshake. "Maybe we can do this again sometime."

As I watched her walk away, I was aware of feeling more…*alive.*

CHAPTER TWENTY-FIVE

Allie and I arrived at Mr. Roberts' house. Once inside, Frank explained that his daughter was unable to be there because she was spending the night with a girlfriend. As he told us this, he looked vaguely uncomfortable, shifting from one foot to the other. I began to wonder if there really was a daughter, given she'd been a no-show at our house as well. But if there wasn't a daughter, why the ruse? To make Allie feel more comfortable with him? And was Frank possibly disappointed I had come along on a dinner originally offered to her alone?

But in the small talk before dinner, Frank seemed interested in me as well as Allie. He asked about my work with the cruise line and how it differed from psychotherapy. It was an intelligent question. "Well," I said, "the differences are hard to explain, but essentially coaching helps a client establish goals and how to achieve them. It's mainly future-oriented. A psychotherapist helps a patient understand how their past has shaped who they are. And unlike coaching, the relationship between patient and therapist is critical—both as a context for self-discovery and as an instrument of change." I didn't like the word, "instrument," so I elaborated. "I don't mean instrument as in microscope or telescope. More like a musical instrument, something that touches your soul."

Frank paused to take in what I'd said and a thoughtful look came across his face. "So am I correct to assume that life coaching is more action-oriented and psychotherapy more insight-oriented."

An oversimplification, but there was truth in what he'd said. "For the most part you could say that, yes."

A light seemed to brighten in Frank's eyes. "But aren't there times when an action undertaken in the context of coaching might lead to insight, and an insight gained in psychotherapy lead to new action?"

I could see why Allie liked Frank so much. He was intelligent, a quick study, and a creative thinker. "Exactly," I said. "Well put."

Frank looked thoughtful again. "So, is being a life coach on a cruise line your life goal, or is it more a way station along the road to something else?"

I'd actually never thought of what I was doing as a "life goal." I'd fallen into it because I became disillusioned with myself as a therapist and also frightened Ricardo might come knocking on my door again. But when I applied the phrase "life goal" to my work as a life coach on a cruise line, I felt smaller than I wanted to be. "Good question," I said. "I've been asking that myself lately."

Frank looked pleased to have connected so well with my own thinking.

"See, Daddy," Allie said. "Isn't Dr. Roberts *smart?*"

Frank laughed and I did, too. "Yes. He is smart."

"And you are too, Allie," Frank said.

"So, tell me more about your time at Mauna Kea," Allie asked Frank.

I remained puzzled by the missing daughter. At a break in the conversation, I asked where I might find a bathroom. Frank directed me down a hallway and as I approached the bathroom, I saw there were two rooms across from it and another room at the end of the hallway, probably the master bedroom. All along the hallway were pictures of a girl, ranging in age from a toddler to a girl of eight or nine. In some of the pictures two adults were also featured. The man in the pictures was Frank. Clearly, he did have a daughter. But why were there not more recent photos? I quietly opened the door to the first room across from the bathroom. There was a desk with a computer, a desk chair, a love seat and two bookcases, lots of pictures of planets and stars but none of people. More telling, no bed. The second room did have a bed, another desk and a chest of drawers, but the books on the desk seemed professional and technical. One was entitled, *Investing For Retirement: A Modern Approach.* The closet door was ajar and I could see several hangars of clothes. But these were the clothes of an older woman, not the clothes of a teenager. I closed this door and opened the door to the room at the hallway's end. It was indeed the master. I shut the door, convinced no teenage girl made any part of this house her home.

I went into the bathroom long enough to flush the toilet and then returned to the family room, determined to find an opening to ask about Frank's daughter. As I sat down, I noticed another picture of Frank's daughter set in a frame by one of the chairs in the living room. Again, she appeared to be eight or nine. Did she no longer live here? Or had she perhaps died in the same accident that had taken Frank's wife? Allie had said Frank's daughter was nine when his wife died. That fit the oldest age of the girl in the pictures. If his daughter died in the boating accident, why would Frank tell Allie she had survived?

Frank invited us to gather around the dining room table, where he served pot roast with vegetables. During the early part of dinner, Frank talked on about what clothes Allie should pack for Mauna Kea, telling her the location would require both cold weather clothes for trips to the summit and warm weather clothes for excursions to Hilo and beyond. There seemed no good time for me to ask about Frank's daughter. Eventually, I decided to just jump in.

"Excuse me, Frank. I got lost looking for the bathroom and went into the two bedrooms along the hallway. I didn't see your daughter's things in either one. Is there another room I didn't see?" The question hung in the air as Frank's expression shifted from annoyance to anger—apparently, he didn't believe I'd gotten lost—and finally to a sudden sadness. He took his napkin and wiped his eyes.

Allie had a bewildered look on her face. When Frank spoke, his voice caught. "Ann…my daughter…" He looked fraught with pain. "…died in the accident that took my wife." He was looking at Allie now.

"Oh no," Allie said, her voice colored with anguish.

I realized Frank was no sexual predator; he was a man coping with unimaginable loss. A man like me. I felt a swell of compassion for him. He had suffered a loss far greater than my own.

"I'm sorry I lied to you, Allie," Frank said. "I thought if you knew it was just me, you'd be uncomfortable coming. Usually, my sister stays here with me, but she's been gone for a month." For moments, the room was so quiet I could hear the refrigerator motor kick in. "You remind me," Frank said to Allie, "very much of Ann. You don't look like her, but who you are is very much like who she was. You're brave like her and inquisitive and smart, and when we talk, I imagine I get to see something of how she might have turned out." He glanced at me and then back to Allie. "I know your father is gone much of the time, so I thought I could be of help to you."

"You have helped me, Mr. Roberts," Allie said. She took a breath, her expression serious. "But I don't like you lying to me."

I understood Frank's attempt to help Allie, but I didn't like it one bit. He was trying to take my place. May have already done so to some extent. I was upset with myself, too, for taking a job where I was gone half the time. If I hadn't been gone every other week these past six years, would Allie still be planning to spend a year away, following in Frank's footsteps to Mauna Kea? I wanted to tell Allie I was sorry, wanted to find out how she really felt about my job with the cruise line, but the kind of heart-to-heart I wanted to have with her, she was now having with another man.

"I'm sorry," Frank said again to Allie. "But I'm glad the truth is out. And I hope you know our time together helps me as well."

Allie looked at Frank with affection. "I didn't know that. Now I do."

I couldn't help but feel I'd lost a piece of Allie to this stranger. She turned to me and I thought she might be about to reassure me about my place in her life. Instead, she said, "Oh, I meant to tell you. I ran into Carlos the other day after school. He said he knew you."

Carlos? The name didn't ring a bell. I gave Allie a blank look.

"An older man," she said. "Your age or maybe a little older. Latino."

Nothing registered.

"He said it had been a while since you saw one other. He said his daughter goes to my school and she heard me talking about going to Hawaii. Carlos said if I wanted to, I could make extra money for the trip by helping out his secretary at his law office."

"What does Carlos look like?" I asked. A rising alarm had reduced my world to the point where the only important thing was her answer to this question.

"Like I said, Latino. Older. Dark eyes, nearly black. Heavy set but not heavy."

"Does he have a scar just above his right eye?"

Allie thought a moment, her eyes narrowing in concentration. "Yeah, I think he does. So, you remember him?"

I worked to steady my breathing. It was reckless to have taken Angela on as a patient again. "I remember him, but his name isn't Carlos. And he's someone you should stay away from."

Frank asked me how I knew this man.

I didn't want to get into it with him. This was between me and Allie. "I think he may be related to a…patient of mine."

Allie looked puzzled and she angled her head to the side. "I thought you weren't doing psychotherapy anymore."

"I'm not. Well, I wasn't. An old patient showed up on one of my cruises and I'm working with her now."

"So," Frank said, "This Carlos meets Allie at school and invites her to work with his secretary to make some extra money. What's wrong with that?"

I was ready to leave. I said to Allie, "Look, we need to go. We'll talk about this at home."

"No," Allie said, the expression on her face as clear and cold as a stop sign. "No more secrets." The look in her eye told me she wasn't going anywhere until she understood what was happening.

Reluctantly, I settled back into my chair. I tried to pretend Frank wasn't there and spoke only to Allie. "I think what Carlos told you might have been a message to me."

"What message?"

"Something like… 'Back off.'"

Allie looked lost.

I told her the basics, how my patient wanted to leave this 'Carlos,' and that Carlos might do anything to keep me from helping her do so, including threatening—or pretending to threaten—her.

"So I'm in danger?" Allie asked, wide-eyed, looking back and forth from me to Frank.

I didn't know what to say. Ricardo had made no actual threat. It occurred to me that if he knew about Allie's plans to study in Hawaii, he most likely knew she stayed with Liz's family the weeks I was at sea. And if not, it wouldn't be hard for him to find this out. I turned to Frank. "You mentioned your sister normally stays here?"

"Yes. Helen. She'll be back tomorrow afternoon."

Do you think Allie could stay with you and Helen next week while I'm at sea?"

"Of course. Why don't you and Allie come over Saturday and meet Helen. I'm sure she won't mind. She loves company."

"I don't think either one of us is really in danger," I said, "but I want to talk to Carlos, just to make sure. Allie, do you still have the number he gave you?"

"The number's in my contacts." She pushed some buttons on her phone and sent it to me.

The thought of Ricardo inside my daughter's phone gave me a chill. "Let's go home," I said. "I'll call this guy and then we'll decide what to do." I stood from the table, telling Frank I appreciated his willingness to help and that I would call if I still wanted Allie to stay with him and his sister next week.

After I'd taken Allie home and she'd gone into her bedroom to get ready for bed, I opened my phone and retrieved the number Allie texted me earlier. I remembered the time years before when I thought Ricardo might have kidnapped her and it turned out she'd just gone to the bay to feel close to her mother. If Claire were here now, she'd be furious with me for endangering our child. I sensed her disapproval as strong and real as if she were in the room.

I dialed the number.

"Hello, Dr. Mason," Ricardo said. "How are you?"

Smooth as ever, still the bull-shitter. "You went to my daughter's school. You asked her to work for you."

"Yes, of course. I would like to help her save money for her time in Hawaii."

It wasn't hard to figure out how Ricardo had found out about Allie's interest in the Hawaii program. I'd mentioned it to Angela in some chit-chat after one of our recent sessions. She must have naively told Ricardo. "You didn't use your real name," I said. "You called yourself 'Carlos.'"

"It is my middle name. You do not remember this? It is on the form I filled out when I saw you in your office. I often use this name with people who are close to me."

I didn't remember Ricardo ever giving a middle name. Nor did I remember asking him to fill out any form. I'd never wanted to work with the man, never intended to work with him for very long and wanted no record of it, so I'd skipped the paperwork. "Ricardo, if you're trying to send me some kind of message, I wish you'd just go ahead and spell it out."

Ricardo sounded genuinely upset. "I am sorry if I offended you by offering to help your daughter."

Could it be true Ricardo simply wanted to help? Angela had told me Ricardo respected me now, was grateful to me. "Look," I said, "if you want to help my daughter, talk to me first, okay?"

"I understand completely, Dr. Mason. I would ask the same courtesy when it comes to Angela."

"The difference is," I said, my voice carrying the anger I felt, "Angela is an adult and Allie is just a child."

"I do not see it this way. To me they are equal. You love one, I love the other."

"So, this *is* about Angela."

I waited for a response, but the line was dead.

CHAPTER TWENTY-SIX

On the way to the port Sunday morning I thought about calling in sick. I didn't like the idea of Allie staying with Frank and Helen, even though I'd liked Helen when Allie and I met her the day before. Allie should be with *me* now, not some science teacher and his sister. But I didn't call in sick, partly because I wanted to talk to Angela on the ship, where we would have time and space apart from Ricardo, and partly because I was beginning to consider quitting my job with the cruise line. I wanted to consider the decision *in situ*.

Once through ship security, I headed to my cabin. Not five minutes passed before Will was at my door. "Wanted to give you a heads-up, buddy. Lynn's been asking about you. Wants to know if you're on board yet."

In the mood I was in, I found Will's cheerfulness grating. "Will, I appreciate your playing cupid, but I've got bigger fish to fry."

"What's going on?"

I felt the small movements of the ship beneath my feet, a sensation I'd come to look forward to as a sign I was about to become untethered from the land. Now, I hated that the ship would be taking me away from home. Away from Allie. "It's a long story. I'll tell you about it after your shift tonight."

Alone in my cabin that afternoon, I thought about where Allie might be at that moment. Probably hanging with Frank and Helen. Would they go out for ice cream on a Sunday afternoon? Take a walk in the park? Watch a movie? These were things Allie and I never did, and suddenly I wanted to do all of them. For too long, I'd taken time for granted, assuming Allie and I had years left to develop our relationship. Instead of using our time together to dig deeper, I'd let our customary routines carry us along.

Standing at the bow of the boat as the ship left shore had always been a favorite ritual. I took the elevator to the top deck and walked toward the front of the ship. Now, as always, throngs of well-wishers stood on the pier or leaned out of balconies of nearby hotels to bid us farewell. The ship plowed slowly through the purple-blue water, making a v-shaped series of whitecaps stretching after it like a wedding veil. Normally, I felt a small thrill of adventure as the ship left port—muted after so many years, so many departures, but still present. Now, I had an urge to jump ship and head home. Impossible, of course.

Later that evening, after we'd docked at Nassau, I checked my watch. It was nearly time for Will to take a break. I took the elevator up to the fifth deck and waved to him as I took a seat at the bar. Lynn was behind the bar, her back to me. When she turned and saw me, her face lit with pleasure. "Hey, Doc," she said. "What can I get you?"

"Just coffee."

Will was playing a jazzed-up blues number—not so loud as to disturb the conversations of the cones, but loud enough to smooth over any awkward silences. He was good at it, a good piano man.

Behind him, beyond the windows that framed him, gently rolling water stretched to a moonlit horizon. Lynn tapped me on the shoulder. I was struck again how plain she appeared—until warmth changed the shape of her eyes and her face took on a mischievous look. "What have you been up to?" she asked. Now she was the most beautiful woman in the room. I asked if she would join me and Will during his break. "I'll have Kate cover for me," she said.

When the three of us were seated together at a little table by the window of the Windjammer, I told Will and Lynn about the latest development with Ricardo, including my recent telephone conversation with him. Not using his real name, of course.

"Something has to give, right?" Will said. "The current situation can't continue."

I took a drink of coffee, set the cup down. "No, it can't."

"So, will you stop seeing that woman—the lawyer's girlfriend?" Lynn asked.

"I could cut her loose after our session tomorrow, then call her boyfriend and tell him I'm done with her. Or, I could call tomorrow and *tell* him I've cut her loose but continue to work with her the remainder of the week. He wouldn't know the difference." A good plan, I thought.

"I don't see the big deal about cutting the girl loose," Will said. "She got herself into this mess. She can get herself out. Or not."

The thought of abandoning Angela again turned my stomach. But Will was right in one respect. Continuing to work with her was out of the question.

Lynn studied my face. "You have a strong connection with this girl."

"I do. I started working with her not long after Claire was killed. After that, my work became even more important than it had been."

"Who's Claire?" Lynn asked.

"She was my wife. Allie's mother."

"Your wife was…killed?"

An image of Claire came to mind. Actually, an image of an image: the way she looked in the picture I still kept in the family room, her blue-green eyes beautiful but impenetrable, her blondish hair falling casually across part of her face. I looked at Will. "You didn't tell her?"

"Not my place, my friend."

"Yes," I said to Lynn. "She was killed in an automobile accident when Allie was nine."

"I'm so sorry." Lynn put her hand over mine.

Should I tell her, I wondered. *And if I do, will she pull her hand away?* "It was my fault," I said, looking down. I looked up again, made myself say it. "I took my eyes off the road." A flash of the instant the semi hit Claire's side of the car caused me to flinch and sent me, for an instant, to that dark place I knew well, a place of unmitigated guilt and shame. Lynn looked over at Will, who remained expressionless. He'd heard it all before. I knew what Lynn's next question would be.

"Why'd you take your eyes off the road?"

I gave her the best answer I could. "My wife—Claire—told me she was thinking about a divorce. I had no idea. And then she said she was seeing someone. That's when I took my eyes off the road and…ran the red light. A semi hit her side of the car."

"God!" Lynn exclaimed, so loudly several people from neighboring tables looked our way. "I'm sorry," she said. "I didn't mean to attract attention. But…you didn't see the light turn yellow?"

A dumb question. Obviously, I hadn't. How many thousands of times had I asked myself that same thing? I didn't answer the question.

"Your poor daughter," Lynn said. "I hate to think of what the two of you went through."

Apparently, Lynn thought Allie and I had borne our grief together. Actually, once Allie found out it was my fault, there were times when she and I dwelled in separate compartments of grief. Things were better now, but I couldn't be sure how much, deep down, Allie still held me responsible. We hadn't had that conversation in a very long time.

There was silence at the table now, as though the three of us had followed a path into a forbidding wilderness and the path had come to a dead stop. Will broke the silence. "So, what are you going to do about the situation with the lawyer guy and your patient?"

"I'm not sure," I said, putting my hands on the little table between us. "But I'm beat. Let's continue this conversation tomorrow, after I've had a chance to talk with my patient."

In my stateroom, I made a quick call to Allie to tell her goodnight. I learned she and Frank and Helen hadn't done anything special after all, just gone to his house where Frank watched sports on TV and Allie did homework while Helen cooked dinner. I had learned something, though, from my fantasy of what Allie might have done with them. In whatever time we had left, I wanted it to be quality time. Together.

I went through my usual go-to-bed ritual: changing clothes, brushing my teeth, flushing with mouthwash, getting into bed. But I couldn't sleep. My heart was with Allie, not on this "stupid boat," as she'd called it. I thought about all I'd learned about her recently:

her interest in astronomical studies at the University of Hawaii, her relationship with Frank. How long, I wondered, had she nursed the Hawaii plan without my knowing about it? And were there other aspects of her life I was completely in the dark about? Probably so.

For most of the night I slipped in and out of sleep, dreaming intermittently of sitting before a board of inquisitors who grilled me about the choices I'd made in deciding to become a life coach on a cruise line. I thought my answers were good. They made sense. But the inquisitors remained unconvinced.

The next morning, I awoke feeling dull-witted and thoroughly pummeled. After having coffee in my room, no breakfast, I took the elevator up to my office for my first appointment of the day. As Angela came through the door, I wondered if she knew about Ricardo's encounter with Allie or my conversation with him. I thought of the advice Wilfred Bion, a British Object Relations theorist, gave for the practice of psychotherapy. He said one should approach each session with neither memory nor desire. But with Angela, I had far too much of both. Desire for Allie and me to be safe. Memory of what had happened the last time Angela and I worked together. Over the years, I'd wondered if there might have been some way I could have continued to work with her. This morning I knew it had always been as impossible as it was now. The sense of menace I'd felt from Ricardo had blurred over time. It was a blur no more. Before Angela had a chance to begin the session, I told her Ricardo had gone by Allie's school and suggested she work for him. Angela's eyes showed disbelief, then alarm. "I think he wanted to send me a message," I said.

Angela gripped the sides of her chair with both hands, her knuckles turning white. "He wouldn't hurt your daughter. I'm sure of it. He meant to scare *me*, not you. He knew you would tell me about his meeting with your daughter. The message…it wasn't meant for you, it was meant for me."

I didn't believe Ricardo's only intent was to scare Angela. And there was something else. "Did he say anything to you about having talked to me?"

For a moment Angela looked confused. "He spoke to you?"

"I confronted him about his meeting with my daughter." I leaned forward in my chair to meet Angela eye to eye. "Angela, if it was only you he was trying to scare, don't you think he would have told you about talking to my daughter? And to me?"

Her eyes widened. "Dr. Paul, there's something you should know."

"What's that?"

"Yesterday I put a deposit down on an apartment. It's perfect for me, a little studio."

I remembered Ricardo had already put the condo where they lived together in her name. I asked her about it. She said it didn't matter whose name the condo was in, Ricardo still acted like it was his. She'd asked him to give his key back and he'd refused. So she found a place of her own.

I didn't quite get why she seemed so alarmed about this. Unless… "Did you tell Ricardo you'd put a deposit down on the new place?"

She shook her head. "No. But I left him a note. He would have seen it either last night or this morning."

"Has he contacted you about it?"

"I don't purchase out-of-country coverage for my cell. Not because of the money. I just don't want to be bothered."

"So, he knows you're planning to leave, and he knows you're here talking with me about it right now."

"Yes," she said, her voice barely there.

I worked to keep the anger out of my voice. "Angela, I need to make sure Allie is okay. We need to end this session." I was already on my feet, moving toward the door.

As she left, Angela looked angry, too. Was she angry because I'd dismissed her so abruptly? Or was she angry with herself for underestimating Ricardo, what he might do? I couldn't worry about that. I entered Allie's number on the keypad of my phone, made a mistake, had to enter it again. It seemed a long time before her phone started to ring, each unanswered ring more agonizing than the one before. When I finally heard her voice, my relief was immediate—until I realized I'd gotten her voicemail. Of course. She was at school. I left a message for her to call as soon as possible. I hoped she might call during her mid-morning break, which had started about fifteen minutes ago. I reminded myself Ricardo didn't know Allie was staying with Frank and Helen now. If he were to tail her after school, or have her tailed, he could find out. But most likely he hadn't done that yet.

I was entering the crew cafeteria when my cellphone vibrated in my pocket. I pulled it out and saw the call was from Allie.

"Daddy?" Her voice was too high and trembly.

"Is something wrong?"

"Yes. Very wrong." She told me that when she stopped by the house to pick up some things during her morning break, things she'd forgotten to get before, she found the front door standing open. Inside, the door to my study was off its hinges. She said the room was a mess—chairs upended, books and papers strewn across the floor. Both her bedroom and mine had been ransacked. She'd called the police, who were on their way.

It was hard for me to keep up with what Allie was telling me, harder still to take it in. "Allie, I'm coming home. I'll book the first flight out of Nassau."

"I'm glad you're coming home, Daddy."

I found Will and Lynn, who were sitting together in the cafeteria for an early lunch. I told them I was headed home. "There's been a break-in at my house."

"What?" they both exclaimed, Will's voice a half-second behind Lynn's.

"Is it related to that woman you're working with?" Lynn asked.

"I don't know. My daughter says the house is a mess. The police are on the way. I'll fill you in later."

I cancelled my appointments for the week and took the first plane from Nassau. During the short, bumpy ride to Miami, the sky so overcast I felt entombed within the passenger cabin, I tried to keep an open mind, to think that maybe this hadn't been Ricardo's doing. There were plenty of break-ins in Miami Shores, and why would Ricardo want to break into my home?

After the plane landed, I called Miami Shores police to ask what they knew. They told me to come by the station. There, I was told the break-in was a professional job—one meant to "send a message." The detective in charge, Detective Day, a short man and razor thin, explained that the perpetrators could have gone in and out without a trace—gotten whatever they'd come for and left. Instead, the door to my office had been deliberately pulled from its hinges and chairs overturned. File cabinets were left with drawers hanging open.

"Whoever did this wanted you to know they were there," Detective Day said. He asked if I had any idea who might have done it.

I remembered what Angela told me years ago about the incident with Ricardo's driver, how Ricardo had made one phone call and the cops let it go. I couldn't trust the police to keep me safe now, and I certainly didn't want to escalate a fight with Ricardo. I played dumb and told the detective I had no idea who it might have been.

When I left the police station it was mid-afternoon. I went straight to my house. Allie was no longer there. Her school was only blocks away; she must have returned there after the police left. Maybe I could catch her before she rode home with Frank.

What I found in the house was hard to believe. Allie's bed was overturned, the mattress slashed. The violence of "the message" was chilling. I lifted the bed frame to set it right and a business card fell to the floor. Printed on the card were the words, "Ricardo Raphael, Attorney at Law." I couldn't pretend now it had been anyone else. My heart raced as I went into my own bedroom. My bed was also overturned, and as I stood in front of it I noticed a tear in the bottom of the box springs. I knelt down and looked closer. Stuffed inside the box springs was a thick notebook. I reached in and pulled it out. It was a journal, and when I opened it and saw the first page of entries, I knew my world would never be the same.

The handwriting was Claire's.

CHAPTER TWENTY-SEVEN

Should I read it? Surely there would be pain in these pages. And what of my own history would I have to revise? Yet how could I not seek to find what had been hidden within Claire's opaque eyes? I sat in a wooden chair in the corner of the bedroom and opened the journal. With its first entry, the years between then and now dissolved into nothing.

03/30/2010 — Nearly cried when A left for school holding P's hand. Whatever is wrong between us, he's so very good with her. I need to remember that.

The date in the journal indicated this had taken place a little more than a year before Claire died. I reread it. *Whatever is wrong between us.* I didn't have a clue what she meant. But the description of me walking out the door holding Allie's hand stirred a longing for that simpler time between Allie and me. Walking with her beside me, her hand tucked tightly in mine, had once been an ordinary, casually treasured event. I thought we would always be this close.

04/05/2010 — Another Easter come and gone. A didn't want an Easter Egg Hunt this year but did it for me. Was surprised P came with me to church today. Don't know what I was looking for, a direction maybe. But sitting next to him in the pew only made me feel worse. And then he criticized me for going.

I remembered this, probably because something about that morning puzzled me. We hadn't gone to church, either of us, since before Allie was born. I was surprised she wanted to go. I searched my memory for the critical comment Claire referred to, or even an unexpressed critical feeling she might have picked up on. What I remembered was being curious. I asked her, after the church service, why she'd wanted to go. Might she have taken this question as a criticism? She must have because she shut down after that and wouldn't talk the whole ride home. Her shutting down had made me angry, and I may well have said something critical then. After the shut-down.

After lunch P ran off to play tennis with R, leaving the dishes to me. Then he called to say he and R were going out to dinner. I told him okay, but how could he have missed the disappointment in my voice? Especially since my first response was "Really?" I only wish he were half as attentive to me as he is to his patients. He acts as if listening is a tool to be used at work but unsuitable for the home.

I leaned forward in the chair. I could understand Claire's sense of being ignored. There were many Sunday afternoons I'd played tennis with Roger, and sometimes we'd gone out for dinner after. I'm sure Claire was right. I'd been so focused on what I wanted to do, I didn't pay much attention to her response. I'd probably heard the word, "Okay," and that was that.

The next few entries were trivial references to mundane events: taking Allie shopping, Claire's thoughts about news of the day, how the rain that spring was never-ending.

Then this.

04/19/2010 — Came home to find P and A playing checkers. Sat down to watch. A so smart, trying so hard. Wish P would let her win. When I told him this later he bit my head off.

I remembered this, too. I did let Allie win once. She'd caught on and was furious about it. "Don't you ever do that again, Daddy," she'd said. So I hadn't. Now, I would like nothing more than to tell Claire that fair play was what Allie wanted. In fact, insisted upon. But how do you argue with a ghost?

04/25/2010 — P critical during dinner. And he wonders why I don't want to have sex with him anymore.

I was skimming the entries now, seeing myself in a new light. Claire's light. Apparently, I'd been so focused on wanting more from her, more transparency, more vulnerability, I became for her a voice far more critical than supportive. There was in her experience of me an ugliness I hadn't seen before. It was hard to look at.

05/20/10 — Saw Dr. T today. I like him. He's a good listener, asks good questions. Wish I'd seen him sooner. He advised couples therapy, but I told him I need to find out where I am before I try to figure things out with P.

"I'm seeing someone." I could almost hear the words. It was a therapist after all, not another man. And I'd over-reacted in the worst way. A wave of nausea hit me and I closed my eyes, breathing slowly, until it dissipated. I closed the journal.

Maybe I shouldn't read any more. But…I opened it again and, dully now, scanned the next few pages. Nothing remarkable.

Until…

06/01/2010 — P tried to be nice to me during dinner tonight. He and A were having fun with the fondue and he tried to include me. I was bitchy in a subtle way. I didn't think P would notice but he did. I should tell him what's going on. It's not fair he doesn't know.

A few pages later:

06/12/10 — Saw G again last night. Told P I was out late with V. Awful to deceive him, but I feel things with G I don't feel with him. He's always trying to reach inside me, demanding I give him more, but G likes me as I am, so I want to give her more. G asked if we could spend a weekend together. Should I? Maybe after Ohio?

I re-read the pages, my mouth dry. Claire *had* cheated on me, after all. I never imagined it had been with a woman. Had I known her that poorly? And who was "G?" I searched through all Claire's friends, but could find no one whose name began with "G." I knew right away who "V" was. Valerie, one of Claire's best friends.

I also knew the reference to Ohio. The Great Ohio Bicycle Adventure. I remembered Claire had planned to fly home Saturday afternoon when the ride was over, but she'd called that Friday to tell me she wouldn't be returning until Monday. Now I knew—or thought I knew—the reason. She'd spent that night and the next with "G."

The deception hit me hard, almost as though it just happened, even though it had been years ago. I looked at the journal and felt I was holding not just some fading pages, but the secrets of Claire's heart. Never had she seemed so transparent. So real. Never had I been so angry with her. I closed the journal again, holding back my grief. I was tired of it, the grieving. I didn't want to go there, even though the "there" was different now than it had been. I knew more about the contours of Claire's heart now, more about where I'd gone terribly wrong. Reluctantly, I reopened the journal. The next pages were full of happy, teenage-like silliness about how wonderful G was, how strong their connection, how good the sex. I was sickened to read it—not only because of Claire's betrayal, but because I could never remember her feeling quite this giddy about our relationship. About me.

The journal entries became shorter, with longer intervals in between. It was hard to get a sense of her in these pages, as though she'd become as elusive to her journal as she had been to me. I turned a page and was surprised to see it was the last one. There were just two entries, the first written the day before her death.

04/14/11 — They say the grass is always greener and now I know this to be true. Living with G would be impossible. The way she treats her kids makes me cringe, and she's lied to me one time too many. One thing I've learned in therapy is that I haven't been fair to P. I didn't let him know how critical his voice had become, the effect it had on me. I think about trying to get back to him, but I could never tell him about my year truly apart. If I told him about G, wouldn't that make him even more critical?

And then, from the morning of the accident:

04/15/11 — Dr. T challenged me today to test P's capacity to forgive, to tell him about G and see what happens. I haven't even told him I'm in therapy, haven't told him I've met with a divorce attorney.

I need to tell him something. Soon.

"I'm seeing someone." I still didn't know whether Claire had been about to reveal her therapist or her lover. Or, for that matter, her attorney. But I did know this: I could have forgiven her. For one absurd moment I even felt a hope for it, as though it were still a possibility.

I closed my eyes and gave myself the luxury of playing out how it might have gone.

I'm seeing someone.

What do you mean?

You know, a lover.

The wrench in my gut. The knife. *How long?*

I don't know, maybe a year. About a year.

Gathering strength to speak. *So…do you want a divorce?*

Do you?

No.

I need to know we can get through this. I can't have you making me pay for my affair.

I lifted my head, eyes still closed.

Claire, I've already paid for it. Paid for it with your distance and disinterest. Paid for it with your silent anger.

I should tell you, I've been seeing a therapist. A good one. Would you like to see him together?

I opened my eyes, looked around the ruined bedroom, my ruined life, and let Claire's journal slip off my lap onto the floor.

CHAPTER TWENTY-EIGHT

In the kitchen, where I'd left my cellphone, I heard the distinctive sound of ducks quacking—the ringtone I'd assigned to Allie's number. I didn't reach the phone in time. *One more ring and I would have made it.* She left a message: "Hey Daddy, I'm on a bench outside the library waiting for Mr. Roberts to finish up. I was thinking maybe you could meet me here at school. I'd like to see you." After a quick trip to the bathroom, I called Allie back to let her know I was on my way. She didn't answer, which was odd. She'd called just minutes ago. I left my own message: "Sorry I missed your call. I'll try to catch you at school. I'm leaving now." I wouldn't be able to tell Allie about Claire's journal. There were things about her mother she didn't need to know.

At the school I went straight to the bench outside the library. Allie wasn't there. I backtracked to the school office and got directions to Frank's room. I made my way there and knocked on the door. When Frank opened it, I asked if Allie was with him, but I already knew the answer. Beyond the door was an empty classroom.

"No," Frank said. "She told me she'd be waiting for me outside the library." I told Frank I'd gone by the library and she hadn't been there. "Let's go look for her," Frank said, putting his hand on my back. "I'm sure we'll be able to find her."

Frank took me by the bench where Allie said she'd be. She still wasn't there. He stopped a passing student and asked if he'd seen a teenage girl waiting by the library. He hadn't. "Maybe she went to the bathroom," I offered, so Frank and I entered the library and Frank knocked on the women's bathroom door.

"Allie, are you in there?" There was no answer. He asked again. Still nothing.

Outside the library, I called Allie again, and again got her voice mail. This made no sense. It had been more than half an hour since I'd left my first message and she still hadn't responded. I left a second message asking her to call and then, thinking of the business card I'd found in my trashed house, punched in the numbers that would connect me to Ricardo. While doing so I told Frank, "I'm calling the attorney, the one my patient wants to get away from." When Ricardo answered, I asked if he knew where my daughter was.

"I do not understand, Dr. Mason." I could hear traffic noise in the background; I'd apparently reached Ricardo in his car. He must be talking through a speakerphone because the reception wasn't great.

"Do you know where Allie is?" I asked again.

"Dr. Mason, what is this about?"

"She was supposed to be at school and she's not here."

"What has this to do with me?" Ricardo seemed far away.

"You were at my house," I said, anger building in my voice. "You ransacked my home."

"Dr. Mason, are you all right?" Ricardo's tone suggested he thought I might have lost my mind. Frank started to walk down the sidewalk adjoining the library, apparently still looking for Allie.

"No, I'm not all right. Look, I assume you've seen the note Angela left for you. The one about her finding another place to live."

"Yes, of course I have seen this note. And I must tell you, I do not like Angela saying things to another man before she says them to me." There was the sound of a horn honking outside Ricardo's car. "It is a violation, no?"

"Ricardo, I can't stop Angela from leaving you, if that's what she wants to do." Frank was walking faster now. Had he spotted Allie?

"Why do you tell me something so obvious?" Ricardo asked. "A child can understand this."

I realized it was futile to talk to Ricardo. If he'd done something to Allie, he would let me know on his own terms, not mine. Or, more likely, he would let Angela know he was using Allie as a pawn in their deadly game. I closed the connection and caught up to Frank, who stood at an intersection of sidewalks. He seemed not to know which way to go.

"How'd you make out with the attorney?" Frank asked.

"Dead end. I'm calling the police."

"Okay. I'll wait a little longer and then head home, see if Allie shows up there."

I got the number for Detective Day and called him. After I told the detective my daughter was missing, he asked when I'd last heard from her. I said it had been almost an hour.

He was incredulous. "She's been missing less than an hour?"

"Yes. But given the way my house was trashed, I think the two events are connected. Plus, I found something of interest on the floor in my daughter's bedroom. A business card. I know who broke into my house. I believe this man may also be responsible for Allie's disappearance."

"Dr. Mason, we should have another conversation. Can we meet at your house? I want to see that business card."

Forty-five minutes later, back at my torn-apart home, I explained to Detective Day my theory about who might have taken Allie, and why. No sense holding back now. The worst had already happened, and Allie needed help. Day took the business card and said he'd ask Miami-Dade police to go have a talk with Ricardo.

• • •

Late Monday afternoon, on the *Allure of the Seas,* Angela decided to swing by Dr. Paul's office to see if he'd been able to contact his daughter. She thought he had overreacted; there was no way Ricardo would do anything to his daughter. She found a note on the door: *All sessions with Dr. Mason have been cancelled due to a family emergency. RCI apologizes for any inconvenience.* Angela's breathing became shallow. The "family emergency" must have something to do with Dr. Paul's daughter. Had Ricardo done something after all? Either way, she had no more reason to be on this cruise. She chartered a private flight back to Miami.

The first thing she did upon landing was call Dr. Paul. What he told her—that his home had been trashed and his daughter was missing—seemed unbelievable. He said his last contact with Allie had been a missed phone call more than an hour ago. He also said he'd found Ricardo's business card underneath his daughter's overturned bed.

"Wait." Angela said now, her eye twitching, "What did you say?"

"Ricardo left his business card under my daughter's bed after he ransacked my house."

Angela had never before heard the word, "ransacked," but its meaning was clear. *Ricardo left a business card?* She wondered if this had been on purpose or an act of carelessness. But Ricardo was rarely careless. Everything Dr. Paul was telling her seemed impossible. And Dr. Paul seemed angry with *her* about it. "I'm so sorry, Dr. Paul," she said, feeling awkward. When Dr. Paul didn't respond, she said "Look, I'll talk to you later" and ended the call. Then she called Ricardo and left a message telling him to meet her at the condo. Immediately. She took a cab to wait for him there.

Ricardo was on his cell as he entered the condo. His hair was disheveled and there was a hard look to his face. When he ended the call, Angela stood and approached him, so close he took a step back. "Where is Dr. Mason's daughter?" Angela asked.

Ricardo shook his head, seemingly bewildered. "Dr. Mason asked me the same thing. Why does everyone think I know where his daughter is?"

"She's missing, Ricardo."

"Yes, so I understand." Ricardo walked past her to the sofa and sat down.

She turned to face him. "Dr. Mason told me you jerked his daughter around, asked her to work for you after school."

Ricardo spread his arms wide and gave her a smile so tight-lipped, Angela thought it must have hurt. "I did not jerk her around. I was trying to help her. I explained this to Dr. Mason."

Angela couldn't believe the gall of the man. She wanted to hit him. "I don't believe you," she said.

Ricardo closed his eyes, let out a breath. "I feel I owe Dr. Mason. He helped me, and I would like to help his Allie."

"This is bullshit, *bull*shit," Angela said, leaning into Ricardo. She put her hand inside the pocket of her jeans and felt the small, aluminum frame of the DoubleTap pistol she'd brought with her. Two rounds. But not yet. She had to find out where Allie was. She tried another tack and sat down beside him.

"I assume you got my note," she said.

"Yes, of course."

"You're not going to try to stop me?"

"How can I stop you, Angie. You are a grown woman."

"You've tried to stop me before."

Ricardo wrapped his hand around his forehead and pulled it slowly down his face, stretching the skin. "*Ay, caramba.* Nobody will believe I have changed." He turned to face her. "Okay, I abducted Allie. I did this to get you to stay with me. Tell me you will do so, and I will let her go." He said this in such a defeated, sarcastic tone, Angela didn't know what to make of it.

She reached into her pocket, put her fingers around the DoubleTap. "Okay," she said. "If it's a trade between me and Allie, where is she?"

Ricardo was looking at the hand in her pocket, the bulge in its middle. "What is this?" He stood from the sofa, eyes wide. "You bring a gun into our home? You wish to threaten me?"

She withdrew her hand. "Just tell me where she is."

"Get out, Angie. Go—before I call the police and have you arrested." He was breathing heavily, shouting at her.

She was about to confront him about the damage to Dr. Paul's home and the business card—*his* business card—found there, when she heard an unusually loud knock on the door.

CHAPTER TWENTY-NINE

Ricardo opened the door to two Miami-Dade cops. Angela had an urge to walk over from the couch and make sure they came in, but she was all too aware of the bulge in the pocket of her jeans, for which she didn't have a permit. It was a mistake to have brought it. She could never kill anyone. Or maybe she could, if Ricardo got her angry enough. Even more reason to have left the gun at home.

Ricardo ushered the policemen into the room and introduced Angela as his girlfriend. One of the policemen was strikingly tall and thin, the other short and squat. They gave their names, but Angela assigned them her own names: "Shorty" and "Tall Boy." Tall Boy asked if she would excuse them while they spoke to "Mr. Raphael," but Ricardo extended a hand toward her, palm down, indicating he wanted her to stay. This was surprising, since she was not exactly a friend in the matter. She remained seated while the other three stood and talked. Tall Boy asked Ricardo if he knew an "Allie Mason." Angela was reassured by this. They'd come for the right reason. She waited expectantly to hear what Ricardo would tell them.

"I have met her, yes," Ricardo said. Tall Boy asked about the nature of their relationship. Ricardo explained that she was the daughter of his psychotherapist, and that he'd met her only once, at her school. Shorty started to take notes.

"Do you know Miss Mason's current whereabouts?" Tall Boy asked. Angela was pretty sure he did know, but she couldn't imagine he would divulge this information.

"I do not." Shorty looked up from his notepad and grimaced.

"Can you tell us the nature of your meeting with Miss Mason at her school?" Tall Boy said.

"I met with her to offer her a part-time job at my law office. She has plans to study abroad—well, not abroad, exactly. In Hawaii. I wanted to help her earn money for her personal expenses."

Tall Boy looked skeptical. "You sought out the daughter of your psychotherapist without his knowledge or permission?"

Ricardo shifted from one foot to the other. "I will be honest with you." Tall Boy and Shorty shared a glance. Angela stood from the couch. "The offer I made was not intended to help her. It was intended to send her father a message." Angela could hardly believe Ricardo was admitting this.

"You mean it was a threat." Shorty said, his own tone threatening.

Ricardo looked down at the officer. "You could call it that. But I would never do anything to hurt the girl. Like I said, it was a message."

Tall Boy spoke. "What was this 'message' you wanted to send to your psychotherapist?"

Ricardo's lip curled as he pointed to Angela. "He was working with my girlfriend. In secret. Do you not think it is a breach of professional ethics for my therapist to be working also with my girlfriend? Behind my back? I simply let him think there might be dire consequences should he continue this practice. Again, I would not actually have harmed the girl."

Tall Boy said, "So you acknowledge threatening the father, but you don't know anything about the girl's whereabouts."

"Yes sir, that is true. I know she is missing. Her father told me as much earlier today. I told him the same thing I am telling you. I know nothing about it. I also know nothing about a supposed break-in at his home. Look, if I had done something to the girl, I certainly would not admit to threatening her father. Which, by the way, I did not do. I simply made a dishonest offer to help his daughter." Angela had to admire Ricardo's ability to take the truth and stretch it beyond recognition.

Ricardo walked to the front door and held it open. "If you have no more questions, I have work to do. Unless…" he offered his upturned fists in mock submission, "you wish to arrest me."

"We do have more questions, sir," Tall Boy said. Ricardo closed the door but remained standing in front of it. Tall Boy presented a business card and handed it to Ricardo. "This was left at Dr. Mason's home—after someone, as you say, broke in."

Ricardo turned the card over, shrugged, gave it back. "Anyone could have left it there. Go to Dr. Mason's house, conduct an examination. If you find my fingerprints there, which I assure you, you will not, then come back and arrest me. Otherwise…" He opened the door again.

Tall Boy and Shorty moved closer to one another and spoke in whispered tones. After a minute or two, Tall Boy thanked Ricardo for his time and said, "I'm sure we will meet again." Then they left.

Angela walked toward Ricardo. “Tell me. Why did you want me here for your little show?”

“It was not a show,” he said, shaking his head. “I wanted you to hear the truth. Yes, I tried to get Dr. Mason to quit working with you by contacting his daughter at her school. But I did not take her.”

“You really don’t know where she is?”

The question seemed to weary him. He sighed and shook his head again. “No. I do not.”

CHAPTER THIRTY

Allie was dimly aware of lying uncomfortably on her side on a carpeted floor. With great effort, she opened her eyes. There was no light. Something covered her eyes, some kind of cloth. *Focus,* she told herself, but it was hard, her mind sluggish. She tried to reach for the cloth covering her eyes, but her hand, no both hands, were bound behind her back. A wave of panic thrust her fully alert and she struggled against the cords. Where was she? She stopped moving and lay there, feeling helpless and electric at the same time. She told herself to slow her breathing, to think, to listen. There was no sound, only a musty, dirty smell she wanted to get away from.

As if reaching for a forgotten dream, she searched her mind. She'd been waiting on a bench looking at something on her phone. How long ago? A man, or men—yes, there were two of them—grabbed her from behind, hurting her. Did she scream? She did fight, she remembered that. But she'd been too surprised, too *taken,* to free herself. A wet and bitter smelling cloth was pressed onto her nose and mouth and then—nothing.

It had all happened so fast. They must have drugged her and brought her here. But why? And who were they? What did they want? She'd been…*kidnapped?* For money? For sex? She forced herself to take a long, slow breath to keep the drowsiness from overcoming her. She pushed herself upright, which wasn't easy with her hands bound behind her. But it was important, to get upright. She stretched out her legs and her feet touched a solid object. A wall. The wall gave a little. Not a wall, a door. A closet door. She scooched backward and found a wall behind her. She was breathing heavily again and too fast, as though inhaling air through a narrow straw. She opened her mouth and took in a slower breath. Momentarily, she had the feeling of being trapped in a mind that was losing control. She couldn't let that happen.

She pushed herself back until she was flush against the wall of the closet. She'd meant to rest there until she could figure out what to do, but as though acting apart from her, her mind began to work again. She recalled her father telling her about 'Carlos,' how she might be in danger from this man. At the time, it had all seemed hypothetical. She tried to remember what Carlos wanted. He wanted to intimidate his girlfriend. And intimidate Allie's father. *She* would be his leverage to do so. If this is what had gone down, wasn't she, in a certain way, important to Carlos? He would want to keep her safe. Wouldn't he?

But he might harm her to some extent, to get his point across. She remembered a movie where the mafia cut off a man's ear and sent it parcel post to the man's father. She had to do something. She placed her head firmly against the wall behind her and by moving her head up and down, tried to dislodge the blindfold. After what seemed like several minutes, but may have been only seconds, it slipped a fraction down her face. She worked harder, shaking her head violently, until the blindfold rested just below her mouth. Beneath the closet door there appeared a faint line of light. It must be originating from a window in the room beyond. She rested her eyes on that light. There was a world out there.

How long had she been here? Not terribly long, because it wasn't dark yet, and she didn't think she'd been kept here overnight. She needed to pee but wasn't desperate. She was hungry, but not famished. So—she hadn't been here overnight. Where were the men who took her? Had they contacted her father? Was he aware of her plight? The thought gave her hope. He would know what to do.

The distant *thud* of a door closing startled her. She heard the faint sound of two men talking. Whatever was going to happen, it would happen soon. There were footsteps and the sound of chairs being pulled across the floor. Were they sitting down at a table? If she kept her breathing quiet, she could make out their conversation.

You think we should contact Ricardo, tell him we've got the girl? A young man. Latino accent.

Let him stew for a while. It'll up our leverage when the time comes. Also Latino. Older.

You sure they'll think it was him who took her?

I made sure to leave one of his business cards at the doc's house.

What do we do with the girl in the meantime?

Get her out, feed her. Let her go the bathroom.

Allie heard another scrape of a chair against a wooden floor and footfalls approaching the closet where she sat huddled. Her breathing quickened and she told herself to keep her wits about her. The footfalls were uneven; the man must have a limp. Here was the moment she'd both wanted and feared, the moment where something would happen. The closet door slid open—*so much light*—and she was looking into the face of a middle-aged, Hispanic man, a face rough and worn. Unpleasant. It was not the face of 'Carlos.'

"Get up," the man demanded, his voice low but with a bite. She realized how scared she was when her legs wouldn't stop trembling as she tried to get them underneath her. Standing wasn't easy, the way her hands were bound behind her. The man watched impassively as she struggled to her feet. Bending low under a dowel meant for hanging clothes, she made her way out of the closet. Now upright, she nearly collapsed from an onset of dizziness. She could see the room was sparsely furnished with a single bed and nightstand, which had a lamp with no shade. The carpet, once apparently white, was discolored here and there with dark streaks. Along one wall was a large window. It was dusk out. Dark clouds filled the part of the sky she could see.

"Follow me," the man said, and he took her to a table in the adjoining room where a younger man sat. The table was wooden and marked with a myriad of scratches, some of them quite deep. The younger man looked at her as though she were a delicacy to be devoured. For some reason, he was wearing blue plastic gloves. She looked away from him and scanned the room. There were only two doors, the one she'd come through and another on an adjacent wall. Beyond this door was a hallway. The older man sat beside the younger and motioned for her to sit in a chair across from them, facing the hallway. A handgun rested on the table beside the younger man. Again, Allie wondered if anyone was looking for her. Surely her father was. But was there any hope he might actually find her?

The men across the table hadn't said anything yet; they were just looking at her. She kept her eyes on the older one. She remembered what she'd heard in the closet, that they were going let her out to eat and pee. "I'm hungry," she said, "And I need to pee."

"Bathroom's through there," the older man said, pointing to the door behind him.

"I can't go like this," she said, raising and lowering her bound hands behind her back.

"I can help you in the bathroom," the younger man said, grinning.

"Shut up, Jose," the older man said. He called Allie to him and took a pocket knife from his pants. He turned her around and cut the cords that bound her hands. This gave her some relief; now she had a better chance of defending herself. She looked again at the gun on the table. She'd never used a gun. Even if she managed to grab it, by the time she figured it out how to work it, they'd have it back. She rubbed her wrists, sore from where the cords had been. "You think about causing trouble," the older man said, "I'll let Jose have you." The old man winked at this, but not in a friendly way.

He pointed the way to the bathroom. His words about the younger man "having her" echoed in her mind as she walked the few steps to the bathroom door. Inside, she took her time, trying to settle herself enough to come up with a plan. She'd been hoping for a bathroom window but there was none. The only way out of the house was back down the hall, in the opposite direction from which she'd come. She thought again about her father; he must know by now she was missing. He probably would have gone to the police, but the police might assume "Carlos" had her. How much time would be wasted chasing down that rabbit hole? She hated the idea of leaving the bathroom to face the two men, but Jose had already knocked on the door and called her name. There was nothing to do but go back and find out what was up. See what they wanted. At least the older man seemed focused on something besides hurting her, and it looked like he was the one in charge.

When she returned from the bathroom, there was a peanut butter and jelly sandwich set on a paper plate on the table. Beside the sandwich was a glass of water. "Eat," the older man said. She sat down and picked up the sandwich. Even though she was hungry, the idea of eating made her nauseous. She forced herself to do so, not knowing when her next opportunity might come. She asked the older man what his name was. He said Luiz. She continued to eat, thinking Luiz would tell her what was up, but he didn't. It struck her that these men seemed to have little more idea how to proceed than she. When she finished the sandwich, she looked at Luiz. "What do you want?" she asked, her voice trembling. She didn't like that. She could not show weakness.

Luiz retrieved a cellphone from his shirt pocket. "You're going to make a call. I think you know Ricardo Raphael. You're going to tell him that Luiz and Jose have you, and then you will return the phone to me. You will say nothing more, only that. Understand?" Jose picked up the gun and pointed it in her direction.

Somewhere beyond her fear, Allie was aware of a building anger. These two men seemed utterly without care about what might happen to her. And why would "Ricardo" be concerned about her? *Should I make a run for it?* she wondered. But she didn't know where a door to the outside was, if it was locked, or what was beyond this house. And there was that gun. She stayed put while Luiz punched numbers into his phone.

"Ricardo, it's Luiz. …No, *you* wait a minute." The cords on Luiz' neck stood out. "There's someone here who wants to speak to you." Luiz handed the phone to Allie.

"It's Allie. Allie Mason," she said. "These men say I know you."

"So that's where you are," Ricardo said. "Everyone has been looking for you."

She recognized the voice as belonging to the man she'd known as "Carlos." She had to remind herself what Luiz had asked her to say. "I'm supposed to tell you that Luiz and Jose have me."

Luiz grabbed phone before she could say anything more. "You hear that?" Luiz asked.

Allie could hear Ricardo's voice through the phone but couldn't make out his words. After a minute or more, Luiz said, "You make us whole—no, *more* than whole—and we give you the girl. Otherwise, she disappears for good and you're in the shit. When we tossed the father's house, we left one of your calling cards. Oh, the police have already come? Yes, so you know. Also, the gun we will use on the girl, if we have to, it is registered to you." As if to illustrate the point, Jose put the gun down and showed Allie the plastic gloves he was wearing—presumably to keep his prints off it.

Luiz was still talking. "Yes, that is what I am telling you. If you look for the gun, you will find it missing. One way or another, you will pay. Either give us what we ask or spend the rest of your life in prison. I call you back in one hour and say what you must do." Luiz ended the connection and nodded to Jose, who was grinning again.

Allie thought about what she'd heard. If this Ricardo didn't give them what they wanted, they were going to kill her. Ricardo, the man her father had warned her about, was now her only hope to survive. She felt a chill and her teeth began to chatter.

• • •

Angela, who'd been listening to Ricardo's side of the conversation, watched him put the phone back in his pocket. She'd never seen him so rattled. "Who was it?" she asked.

He practically snarled his response. "Two nobodies I cut out of a deal and now they want their share. More than their share. They have Allie, and if I do not do what they say, they will kill her."

"How do they know about your connection with her?"

"They were close to me once, to my…business. They helped me find where Allie goes to school. They know I met with her there."

Angela wanted to ask what Ricardo planned to do, but he'd already left the room. She followed him into his study, where he took a key from his pocket and unlocked a large, brown briefcase. Looking inside, he began to swear in Spanish. "They took my gun," he said. "It is as they say: they will use my gun against the girl if I do not do what they demand, and I will be blamed for her death."

"What do they want?"

He started pacing around the room. "Money, obviously. A lot of it. Maybe more than that. They will call in one hour to let me know."

"How do you know they won't kill the girl after you pay them off?"

Ricardo stopped pacing and pointed to the bulge in the pocket of Angela's pants. "I need to borrow your gun."

"It's only got two rounds."

"Two is all I need."

CHAPTER THIRTY-ONE

It was full dark out and too cold not to have a jacket on when Allie stepped outside the house where she'd been confined. Her hands were bound behind her again and it was difficult to walk. Not just because of the cords; she was shivering uncontrollably now. Moving more slowly than her captors would have liked, she tried to memorize her surroundings in case she might have to describe them to police. The neighborhood was run-down, with small palm trees in nearly every yard, palmettos, and a ragged hedge along the sidewalk. She looked back at the house and saw it was somewhere between burgundy red and rust-colored. The number 721 was attached in fading white letters to the front of the home, beside the front door. She committed the number to memory, hoping to grab the street name later.

Luiz was in front of her and Jose, with the gun, behind. Both men scanned the surroundings like wary rats. When they reached the street, Luiz opened the front passenger door of a beat-up Toyota Camry and told her to get in. Jose got in behind her and Luiz walked around the front of the car to take the driver's seat.

Allie figured it had been no more than two or three hours since she'd been let out of the closet. Luiz had called Ricardo a second time, but she hadn't heard what was said because he'd made the call from another room. She'd gathered from the conversation between Luiz and Jose afterward that they were now on their way to meet with Ricardo. She thought this meet could well go very wrong. She looked up as they passed a street sign at the corner, trying desperately to make out the name. It was too dark see anything but a double "e." Would that be enough for the police to go on? A double "e?" Was there any chance she would even be in a position to talk to the police? She didn't see how.

Luiz and Jose weren't talking but she wished they would; her legs were still trembling and she needed the distraction. Plus, it might give her something to go on, some clue as to where they were going or what would happen next. She thought about asking Luiz where they were headed, but somehow it didn't seem her place. She was a hostage. And what did it matter anyway? There was nothing she could do about it.

She couldn't keep track of their route. They made a number of turns, both right and left, but still seemed to be in the same general neighborhood. Then they crossed some train tracks and she could tell they were moving through a commercial area scattered with warehouses. After twenty minutes, or it might have been only ten, Luiz pulled the car to the curb and shut down the engine. Were they at the rendezvous point already? If so, there was no more time ahead of her to push her worry into. The time was *now*.

Luiz got out of the car, came around and opened her door. She didn't budge. Couldn't she just refuse to participate? Luiz took one look at her, leaned in and pulled her roughly out, cursing in Spanish.

Her left shoulder and right foot were hurt, her shoulder pretty badly. Resisting had been a stupid idea. Once out of the car, as she tested her right foot to see if she'd be able to walk, she worked hard again to memorize her surroundings.

They were on a darkened street with no traffic and—surprisingly—no street lights, even though she could see I-95 in the distance, a river of light with its unbroken stream of cars and trucks. *Cars and Trucks and Things That Go,* her favorite childhood picture book. She wished she could go somewhere now. Anywhere but here. Luiz and Jose walked quickly again, in spite of Luiz' limp, one pushing, the other pulling her toward a grey cement building forty or so yards across an empty lot. She'd never imagined there was such a forlorn place as this in all South Florida. It seemed to exist in a world apart: dark, deserted, run-down, yet within sight of so much light and life. It was all unreal.

As they approached the building, she wondered if Ricardo would already be there. *Please be here,* she thought. *Let this be over.* But...what if he didn't show up at all? Would she have to go through all this again? Or would they... She couldn't think about it.

Luiz and Jose led her around to the back of the building. A vehicle was parked there, a black SUV with two men inside. Was one of them Ricardo? No, the men got out and greeted her captors in a way that let Allie know they were friends. These men were dressed in camouflage, like in the Army, and each one carried an automatic rifle. Allie wondered if Ricardo would bring men of his own, with guns of their own. Would there be a shootout? Might she have a chance to escape? She began to have an involuntary tremor in her stomach, a clenching. She replayed the past several hours. Had there been a point when she could have escaped? She couldn't think of one. But if she'd known then what she knew now, she would have tried.

When she and the four men returned from the back of the building, she no longer had to be pushed or prodded. She walked among the four men like a robot. Better not to think at all. Not to feel. Luiz held up his hand. "We wait here," he said, and the other three stopped. After what seemed like half an hour, but might have been only ten or fifteen minutes, the men became bored, resting on one foot and then the other. Allie tried to concentrate only on her breathing. In and out. In and out. If she were shot, what would it be like? Would she feel where the bullet entered? How long would it take her to die?

Slowly, a car approached, a black Mercedes, and Allie's captors became alert. Allie's heart dropped when she saw there was only one passenger. It had to be Ricardo. By himself, he would be as helpless as she. The car stopped and the man she'd known as "Carlos" stepped out the driver's side door, carrying in each hand a large, brown duffel bag. She'd gotten the impression Ricardo was wily and streetwise, but he'd come to this meeting alone and unprepared. She wanted to scream at him. *You idiot!* He stopped maybe fifteen yards away and set the bags down. "I have your money," he said to Luiz. "Let the girl go." He said it politely, seemingly unaware of the danger of the situation. They would never let her go. She was a witness; she could testify against them.

Should she run across the small space between her little group and Ricardo? Or try to run away? But the two men with guns were already raising them. A sense of disbelief that any of this could be happening gripped her mind. She started shaking her head back and forth. *No. No.* Luiz looked at one of his men, the larger of the two, the one with the scruffy moustache, and nodded his head. Allie's disbelief was like an anesthetic now, numbing every nerve. Every thought. Ricardo reached into a coat pocket and pulled something out. It was a pistol, a tiny, pitiful thing.

Allie expected Ricardo to be riddled with bullets from Luiz' men; she braced herself for it. Instead, Ricardo fired the little pistol twice, POP! POP! and both Luiz and Jose fell to the ground. Even as he fell, Luiz had a surprised expression on his face. Allie looked at the men with automatic rifles, sure they would kill Ricardo. The two men turned and fired twice each into Luiz and Jose, their bodies jerking with each hit. Jose made an animal, grunting sound after the first shot, nothing after the second. Without a word, the men with automatics took Ricardo's bags and disappeared behind the building as images haunted Allie's mind: Ricardo firing his little pistol, Luiz and Jose falling, being shot again, convulsing on the ground.

Ricardo approached her with a pocketknife. She didn't understand. Was he going to hurt her? He must have seen the terrified look in her eyes because he held his hands up and spoke calmly. "Allie, do not worry. I am not going to hurt you." He moved behind her and cut the cords binding her hands. "Come with me," he said, holding one hand out to her. "We must get away from this place."

Allie couldn't move. Too much that wasn't supposed to happen had happened already. Luiz and Jose lay lifeless on the ground not ten feet away, blood pooling around Luiz. "Allie, *now,*" Ricardo said, the urgency in his voice jolting her to life. She didn't take Ricardo's hand but ran with him back to the Mercedes. He held open the passenger door and she climbed inside, then he came around and took his place in the driver's seat. She didn't have a clue what had just happened.

"Are you all right, Allie?" Ricardo asked as he drove away. "Did they hurt you?"

"What just happened?" she asked.

"Luiz is not a smart man. I know who he goes to for an operation like this. I reached out to one of the men. I asked him what Luiz offered. He told me and I offered more. The second man was happy to go along, so..." Ricardo smiled as he said this, as though this kind of thing was not foreign to him at all.

"Where are you taking me?" Allie asked, not knowing what might be in Ricardo's mind. Was she *his* hostage now?

"To your father, of course."

To my father? The idea she was no longer a hostage felt unreal, just as becoming a hostage had seemed unreal not that long ago. She looked over at Ricardo. He seemed in a hurry, the expression on his face serious. "What is it?" he asked.

"Nothing," Allie said. "I just..." She let herself sink into the seat of the car and, to herself, finished her thought...*didn't think I was going to make it out of there.* She couldn't stop herself from crying, quietly, as she relived the entire ordeal: being roughly grabbed from the bench outside the library, coming to in the closet, riding to a forlorn place in the city where someone *had* to die. Luiz and Jose shot, a smirk on Ricardo's face as he pulled the trigger. Twice. The surprise on Luiz' face as his legs gave way. She would never forget it, a man meeting death with the surprised expression of a child.

CHAPTER THIRTY-TWO

All I could think of was Allie, where she might be, what she was going through. Detective Day had called to let me know Miami-Dade police had interviewed Ricardo and learned nothing. Of course they hadn't learned anything; Ricardo would never tell them what he'd done. Day assured me they were still "working the case." I considered calling Angela to find out where Ricardo lived so I could pay the man a visit. Maybe if he were looking at the barrel end of a gun, he would be more forthcoming.

Of course, I didn't own a gun, and in that kind of escalation Ricardo would have a clear advantage. I methodically began putting my house back in order, keeping my focus on the next small task at hand. I moved the mattress away from my overturned bed so I could grab the frame and set it right again. As I lifted the frame off the floor, my eye caught Claire's journal, still lying where I'd dropped it. I thought of all that had been unfinished between us, all I could have addressed had I known then what I knew now. I lifted the bed frame high enough so that it fell with a thud upright on the floor. I resolved that if I ever got another chance with Allie, I didn't want anything left unfinished between *us*. I considered the recent shift in our relationship, how it happened because I'd made myself more available. How stupid to have misunderstood her all these years, thinking she didn't want to be close because I had caused her mother's death. I grabbed the box spring by its handles and wrestled it onto the frame of the bed. I resolved that never again would I let my own, miserable fear come between me and Allie. If she wanted to spend the better part of a year in Hawaii, I would support the hell out of her doing so. I prayed I would have the chance.

My cellphone rang. When I saw the call was from Ricardo, my heart jumped.

"I have Allie," Ricardo said. "I will bring her to you." Finally, the man was ready to make a deal. "I am not the one who took her," he added, as though reading my thoughts. "I am the one bringing her back. Do not forget this. And do not involve the police. If there are police present, I will pass you by."

Ricardo hadn't taken her? I didn't believe it. The man couldn't be trusted to tell the truth. I considered calling Detective Day, in spite of what Ricardo said. Surely the police could manage to stay out of sight. But I decided to wait, see what happened, and forty long minutes later a car pulled up to the house. I was halfway to the black Mercedes when Ricardo stepped out, walked around the front of the car and opened the passenger door. As Allie ran toward me, I saw both the fifteen-year-old teenager she was now and the five-year-old little girl who used to greet me this way when I returned home from a long day at the office. I took Allie in my arms and she held on with surprising strength.

She pushed back from me a bit to look at me. "Daddy," is all she said before pulling me to her again. I felt her need of me in a way I hadn't felt in many years. I didn't let her go until I felt her begin to breathe normally again. By that time I was washed out, but with a heart so full it actually felt heavy in my chest.

When Allie and I let one another go, I noticed Ricardo standing a short distance away. Despite the fact he'd brought my daughter home, I was not happy to see the man. With his eyes, he gestured toward my house and I let him in. I owed him that much. Besides, I wanted to know what had happened. I offered Ricardo a spot on the sofa. Allie and I sat together at the other end, Allie sitting close, her hip touching mine, one hand cupping my shoulder. "What's going on?" I asked Ricardo.

Ricardo looked at me with a steady intensity. He explained what had happened to Allie and then said, "What I have done for your daughter has cost me tens of thousands of dollars. Now you will repay me." Ricardo looked at Allie. Twosome entered the room and leaped into her lap. Ricardo asked if we could talk in private.

I asked Allie if she wanted to go or stay. "I'd rather stay," she said, her voice low but firm. I gestured for Ricardo to continue.

"You must stop seeing Angela."

My stomach tightened. I didn't like being told what to do. Especially not this. "And if I don't?" I asked, though my heart wasn't in the question. I'd already made the decision not to work with Angela any longer.

"I assure you, Dr. Mason. This matter is of utmost importance to me. Whether Angela leaves me or not is strictly between the two of us. There will be no outside interference." When I didn't respond, Ricardo added, "Do you understand?"

"I would like to see Angela one more time."

Ricardo frowned. "For what purpose?"

"It's how we do it in my business. If I decide I can no longer work with someone, there must be a termination session."

A look of disgust came across Ricardo's face. "It is you and I who must decide what to do, not you and Angela. That is how *my* business works."

I took a deep breath. "Look Ricardo, I get it that you don't want me to work with Angela, but think of this: if you allow her one final session to bring things to a close, do you think that will help or harm her attitude toward you?" I had no idea what Ricardo was thinking behind those black, intelligent eyes.

"As you wish. One session more."

• • •

Allie and I shared a makeshift meal of garbanzo bean soup. As we ate, Allie walked me through the details of her abduction and rescue and the shock of seeing two men gunned down in front of her. It was hard to hear. I hated that she'd been terrorized, and I knew aspects of that terror would be with her the rest of her life. I would of course suggest she talk to a therapist. But now she was talking to me, and I welcomed every word.

"I feel funny about Luiz," Allie said. "He protected me from Jose, so I feel bad about the way he died. But I know he *had* to die if I was going to live." The expression on her face gave me a sense she thought it was wrong to feel the way she did.

"Feelings are like that, sometimes," I said. "They don't always play well together." The way Allie lifted and cocked her head, with a surprised but knowing expression in her eyes, let me know my remark hit home and that she found it helpful. Nothing could have pleased me more.

After dinner we sat on the same sofa where Ricardo had sat a few hours ago. "I've been thinking," I said. "If you want to spend your junior year in Hawaii, I'm all for it. I'll support you one hundred percent."

"I've been thinking too," Allie said. "I'd like to see the setup in Hawaii, and I'd like you to come see it with me. Maybe we could go over spring break?"

Her wanting to involve me in her Hawaii adventure—me and not Frank—nearly brought tears to my eyes. "I'll make a vacation request with RCI for the week of Spring break," I said, steadying my voice. "I'd very much like to go to Hawaii with you."

"It's not just that," Allie said. Moments passed before she spoke again. When she did, her voice was tentative and small. "Do you think you could get another job?"

Another job? "Don't you like the time you spend with Liz and her family?"

"I do like it. But I'd like it more if you were here all the time." Allie's face took on a hardened look. "I'm sorry if that lets you down."

I leaned toward her and again had to fight back tears. "Allie, how? How would that let me down?"

She leaned away. "You always wanted me to be, you know... *strong.* Especially after Mom died. She paused and looked at me in a suddenly opaque, Claire-like way. "And I am strong. But not all the time." She seemed a little angry.

I was confused. "Allie, what do you mean I wanted you to be strong?"

"Remember how you always told me, when you dropped me off at Liz's, 'Be strong?'"

I remembered. It was a goodbye ritual, something I'd said the first few months I worked for the cruise line: *Love you. Be strong.* But these were words meant as much for me as for her. I recalled the question she'd asked a minute ago, "Do you think you could get another job?" She might as well have asked, "Do you think you could be a better Dad?" But why was she angry? She must not like it, needing me. Or maybe she didn't like how I'd made her spell it out so explicitly, as if to a two-year-old. "Yes, I can get another job," I said, quickly. I thought of my recent work with Angela, how it had connected me to a part of myself I'd lost touch with. I'd been living these last years like a plant in a too-small pot. Withering more than growing.

"You can?" Allie said, surprised. It was as though she'd asked for something impossible, like to live in a golden castle, and I'd said sure, that'd be fine.

"I have to go back to the cruise line for one more week. There are arrangements I need to make. People I need to say goodbye to." *A termination session.*

"Okay," Allie said, a look of relief coming over her.

A line from the Bob Dylan song came to my mind. *Well it ain't no use to sit and wonder why, babe, ifin' you don't know by now.* The song was about a breakup, not a reunion, but that line fit perfectly how I felt: utterly befuddled by what had just happened in the most important relationship of my life.

CHAPTER THIRTY-THREE

Standing on the upper deck of *The Allure of the Seas* as it sailed out of Miami, I felt a sense of melancholy. When I returned to America this time, it would be for good. I'd already secured office space in a professional building in Miami Shores for a private practice, and the money I'd saved over the years would give me time to rebuild a practice. When I'd notified the cruise line's Human Resources Department of my intent to resign, the head of the department offered me more money to stay on, but I turned her down. I'd have to pay a penalty for the premature termination of my contract, but it would be worth the additional time with Allie. This would be my last cruise.

That afternoon at the Schooner Bar, after I'd sat at a little table next to a window, Lynn came over and asked me what I wanted to drink, putting her hand on my shoulder as she did so. I told her I wanted a beer, my usual, and she gave me a wink as she walked away. The chemistry between us was obvious and bittersweet. The decision I'd made would not be without regret. Will noticed me from the piano and took his right hand off the keyboard to give me a smile and a wave. This simple gesture brought a film of tears to my eyes.

For six years I'd worked this ship and only now, after I'd decided to leave, had I found something like family here.

Ain't no use to sit and wonder why, babe...

When Will's set was finished, he joined me at the little table. Lynn came over, too, and looked us up and down. "My two favorite boys," she said. I told them I'd like to get together later that evening, after they finished their shifts, and they agreed to meet me in the crew bar at eleven.

I went to my stateroom and looked over my schedule for the next day. As usual, Monday was a light day. It generally took a while for passengers to learn about my presence on board, even longer to discover they needed my help. I had only three appointments, none of which were Angela; she would be my first patient in the new office. I still hadn't decided what to do about her. I didn't want to abandon her again, but neither did I wish to antagonize Ricardo.

I was seated at one of the tables when Will and Lynn entered the crew bar a little before eleven. After greetings were exchanged, I told them this would be my last week with the cruise line.

Will looked confused, but Lynn's response was immediate. "You're serious, aren't you. I see it in your face. And here I was ready to throw myself at you, consequences be damned."

"Are *you* serious?" I asked.

"Why, you'll never know now, will you?" The look in her eye was playfully seductive. But when her face relaxed, I could see her disappointment.

Will looked distressed. "What will you do?"

I told them about my intention to open a private practice in Miami Shores. I looked at Lynn. "My daughter asked me to quit my job with the cruise line to stay home with her. It surprised the hell out of me."

"Why?" Lynn asked.

"Ever since her mother died, Allie's kept a certain distance. Or I thought she had. I'm not so sure anymore. It may have been more me than her." I told Will and Lynn about the events of last week, how Allie had been kidnapped and we were both confronted with the possibility we might not see one another again. As I told the story, at some remove now from the events themselves, I thought how easily things could have gone another way.

The remainder of the week passed quickly, the sentimental aura surrounding my relations with Will and Lynn growing deeper as the time came for me to make my final deportation. Late Saturday night I considered asking Lynn if she might be willing to leave the boat and find a job in Miami, but I realized to do so would be premature. We didn't really have a relationship, only the promise of one.

Sunday morning I awakened before dawn, the ship having docked during the night. I looked out my small window at the lightening sky and thought about the life I was leaving behind, a cocoon that had insulated and protected and kept me safe for a future I'd never imagined. I would miss it, this life, even as I knew I could never go back.

Later, in the frantic bustle of passengers departing, I searched for Lynn, wanting to tell her goodbye, to let her know how much I liked her, but she was neither in her cabin nor in the Schooner Bar. I did find Will, who told me that on his next leave, he would look me up in Miami Shores. "Maybe I'll get you to give me some of that therapy crap," he said, laughing. "Or maybe just a cold beer."

A little before noon I left the ship for home, anxious to see Allie, who was already there. I'd brought her a gift from one of the islands: a white necklace made of tiny shells. I intended it to be a tangible symbol of the turn our relationship had taken. I wouldn't tell her that because more and more I thought the turn was mine, really, not hers.

When I came through the door, Allie was sitting on the couch with her feet up, talking on the phone with Twosome beside her. I waved to her, but even though she'd clearly seen me, she didn't wave back. She continued to talk animatedly on the phone while absent-mindedly stroking Twosome. As though I wasn't there at all.

Typical teenager. It was Claire's voice. I hadn't heard it in a long time and even after all these years, I missed her still. I shook my head and sat down on the other end of the sofa from Allie, letting my suitcase drop to the floor.

"Are you all right?" Allie had ended her phone conversation and was looking at me with concern.

"I'm okay. Just a rough day." *No,* I thought, *I want more truth between us going forward.* "Actually," I said, turning to meet her eyes, "I was missing your mother."

Allie stood and moved closer to me on the couch. "Aww, I'm sorry," she said and put her head on my shoulder.

• • •

The next day was my first in the new office. It wasn't as large as my old one, but unlike my office on the cruise ship, I'd filled it with things that meant something to me, including two pictures of Allie: one as a six-year-old girl smiling into the camera and one taken yesterday, with Allie wearing the necklace of shells I'd brought her from the islands.

Last week aboard ship, I'd spent several marathon sessions online completing the continuing education credits required to reactivate my license. I wasn't there yet; the State still had to finish its end of the paperwork. In the meantime, thanks to a fairly liberal Florida law, I could still practice. I just couldn't call myself a licensed therapist.

Angela had already arrived—I'd heard her ring the bell ten minutes ago. I opened the door to the waiting room and was taken aback to see Ricardo sitting there. Alone. I didn't try to hide my surprise.

"May I come in?" Ricardo asked, politely. I showed him into the office, where we took seats across from one another, my stomach churning. Whatever Ricardo was here for, it couldn't be anything good.

"I know I am the last person you wanted to see today," Ricardo said. "But I come at Angela's request. She didn't want to face you with…well, let me back up. I am divorcing my wife. I have agreed for Angela to go back to school, and to get a job if she likes. On her own, not with my people. Given these concessions on my part, she has decided to stay with me."

I couldn't believe what I was hearing. Ricardo was divorcing his wife? Letting Angela go to school, get a job? And she wanted to stay with him? "I don't believe you," I said.

Ricardo held out his phone, offered it to me. "Call her. She will tell you herself."

I waved Ricardo's phone away, took out my own and punched in Angela's number. When she answered, I said Ricardo was in the office telling me she'd decided to stay in the relationship. "Is that true?"

"I didn't come today because I didn't want to see the disappointment on your face."

My concern was whether she might be disappointing herself with this decision. "Tell me more about your decision to stay with him."

"Ricardo is…different now. He left his wife. I'm back in school. He's letting me be…*me.* Well, most of the time. Much more than before. And I've been with him so long now it's like he's a part of me."

"I remember," I said. "The teddy bear."

She didn't respond.

"I have to say," I told her, "I would feel better about this if we could have a chance to talk about it in person." Still nothing. "It's important we have a final session to bring our work together to an end. To say goodbye."

"Goodbye, Dr. Paul."

The connection was gone. There would be no opportunity for me to assess, person-to-person, the extent to which she had or hadn't thought this through, or to measure the strength of whatever ambivalence she might have. No opportunity for me to tell her how much she meant to me or how she'd helped me reclaim my own life.

"Will that be all, Dr. Mason?" Ricardo asked.

I couldn't read him. Was he smug with victory or contrite in acknowledgement of his past failings? Maybe both. I looked at him a long time, thinking of all that had passed between us. I still didn't like the man.

"Yes, that will be all," I finally said, and watched Ricardo silently stand and walk out the door.

CHAPTER THIRTY-FOUR

Five Months Later

I looked down at a river of crimson that stretched to the horizon. Only two hours ago, in Hilo, these same clouds had been chalky white at the top of the sky. Allie leaned into me for warmth as a strong wind buffeted us both. It was past sunset, and the temperature at Mauna Kea was falling fast.

"This is not where most girls your age would want to spend spring break," I said.

"Thank you for coming," she said, shivering.

The observatory complex with its telescopes and technology was utterly foreign to me, and the stark landscape here at the top of the sky seemed devoid of life. Yet it was Allie's dream to be here. She'd been accepted into the summer program—a little over two months away now, and I had no doubt she'd want to stay the full year if given a chance. I would have to learn to live alone again. At that thought, I took in a long breath and let it go. I would cross that bridge when I came to it, just as I had crossed many bridges already.

I wondered if Allie and I would be standing here at all had Claire not left us when she did. Certainly not. The confluence of Claire's death and then Allie being told the entire planet would someday perish—this had powerfully affected her young mind.

"Look," Allie exclaimed. I followed her pointing finger across a darkening, star-salted sky. So *many* stars. I wasn't sure exactly what she was wanting me to see, so I moved my head closer to hers to get a better read on where she was pointing. "See there?" she said. "See it moving across the sky?"

I saw it, a tiny dot moving nearly imperceptibly against the constellations of stars.

"It's the International Space Station," she said. "There are *people* up there."

"Yes, I see it. Do you think you might want to go there someday?" The thought of her contained within that celestial speck gave my stomach a lurch.

"Oh, *yes,*" she said. "It'll be different by then, though. Way updated."

I understood her excitement, even though I didn't like it. She was all about helping prepare for getting beyond planet earth and its eventual demise. For her, this had always been something real, not to be dismissed. When she turned to me again, she must have been able to tell I was already missing her because she shook her head. "You can't think that way, Daddy. It's just the opposite. I'll take you with me. You and Mom both." She put one hand on her heart, as though saying the pledge of allegiance.

This gesture and her words touched me. I put my arm around her and pulled her close as we both looked into a sky that stretched on and on. I remembered Allie telling me once about a theory that the universe is bounded, that there is an edge even to infinity. Her life reached there, I knew, toward that edge and a search for habitable worlds yet unknown, even as my life reached to the world below, within and beneath the billowing clouds now turning ruby red.

That world held mysteries, too.

I'd learned something from the accident that took Claire's life, learned how some things cannot be gotten over but must be absorbed, over weeks and months and years. Learned that one must find a way to live within the heartbreak of loss, yet beyond it, too. This learning had enriched my work with patients; I was grateful to be a therapist again. Grateful, too, to have discovered my place in Allie's heart was well anchored. I looked forward to becoming a part of her future as she would become a part of mine.

Allie put her arm around my waist and we turned to walk back toward where my car was parked. The sun had set, the cold dug in for the night. Walking quickly now, I felt my phone vibrate in my pocket. I took it out to see who might be calling. It was a FaceTime call, and on the screen of my phone was the rather plain face of Lynn Smith. We'd kept in touch, a little, and I knew her contract with RCI was nearly up. The last time we'd emailed, she hadn't decided whether or not to renew.

"Hello, Lynn," I said.

"Hi, Paul." A twinkle appeared in her light brown eyes. "I'm coming ashore in two weeks. For good, actually. How about we get together?"

Another thing I'd learned with Claire was that what fills the heart can also break it. And what about Allie? If Lynn and I were able to make something work together, would Allie feel displaced or think I was somehow betraying Claire? I looked at Allie, walking beside me. I couldn't risk hurting her.

I was about to tell Lynn no, I didn't think it was a good idea, when Allie's voice surprised me. "Don't be an idiot, Dad." She rolled her eyes.

I laughed out loud. What fills the heart can break it, yes, but my broken heart was open now. There was room in there.

"Paul?" Lynn asked, her voice uncertain.

I realized she might have thought I was laughing at her or at her invitation. "I'm sorry," I said. "I wasn't laughing at you. Yes, I'd like to get together." I pointed the phone's camera toward Allie. "Lynn, I'd like you to meet my daughter, Allie."